LUCK IN THE GREATER WEST

LUCK IN THE GREATER WEST

DAMIAN McDONALD

Quercus

First published in Great Britain in 2008 by

Quercus
21 Bloomsbury Square
London
WC1A 2NS

Copyright © 2007 by Damian McDonald

Originally published by ABC Books in 2001 for the
Australian Broadcasting Corporation, GPO Box 994
Sydney NSW

The moral right of Damian McDonald to be
identified as the author of this work has been
asserted in accordance with the Copyright,
Designs and Patents Act, 1988.

All rights reserved. No part of this publication
may be reproduced or transmitted in any form
or by any means, electronic or mechanical,
including photocopy, recording, or any
information storage and retrieval system,
without permission in writing from the publisher.

A CIP catalogue record for this book is available
from the British Library
ISBN 978 1 84724 404 8

This book is a work of fiction. Names, characters,
businesses, organizations, places and events are
either the product of the author's imagination
or are used fictiously. Any resemblance to
actual persons, living or dead, events or
locales is entirely coincidental.

Printed and bound in Great Britain by Clays Ltd, St Ives Plc

10 9 8 7 6 5 4 3 2 1

For my child, born August 2007

PART ONE

ONE

Patrick White — Whitey to the customers of his small business situated in Rooty Hill in the western suburbs of Sydney — mixed the Glucodin with the amphetamines, roughly one part to two in favour of the goey. From the cereal bowl he weighed and bagged the mix into quarter, half, and one gram zip-locks. It was pension day, and customers from the Housing Commission estate in Colyton would be crossing the highway to score. Colyton and Rooty Hill lay on either side of the highway. Colyton was a newer development: in brick; but Rooty Hill offered larger houses in fibro and weatherboard.

Like chainsaws had done to the eucalypts that once reigned here, the highway sliced through the outer-western suburbs. There was an overpass ostensibly linking Colyton and Rooty Hill, enclosed with welded mesh to prevent kids and teenagers from killing motorists with half-bricks, but the bridge was too far east of Whitey's place or the big cut-price bottleshop, Booze World, to be convenient for the customers of these and other businesses. All day and night there was a corridor of metal and alloy streaming through, and past, the twin Housing Commission estates. A smaller stream of flesh and bone would wait for breaks in the traffic and cross it. There had been fatalities; collisions and explosions of flesh, bone, metal and alloy, leaving dark patches on the asphalt — kangaroo, dog, cat, and welfare recipient.

There was a shopping mall in Mt Druitt, the next suburb to the west of Rooty Hill. The supermarket, auto banks, bottleshop and, of course, Welfare Centre branch were patronised by the tenants of Colyton and Rooty Hill, but the rest of the retail outlets targeted their marketing to the east, north, south, and further west to the mountains. Rooty Hill had its own smaller shopping precinct that was misleadingly referred to as a plaza. Mt Druitt was a mostly private housing suburb except for a wall of some five hundred Housing Commission flats on its eastern edge, closest to Rooty Hill. Whitey didn't have many customers from here, as there were always plenty of dealers among the flat's transitory tenantry.

People were lucky in the western suburbs. They were housed. They had access to decent food and fresh water. They could indulge in stimulants of pleasure and they could numb themselves. But they were also at the bottom of a bowl of land, parched by having too much of its flora stripped from it, and rimmed by the bright and exclusive northeast that made up Sydney and its inner suburbs, and the lush range of nature and culture further southwest that rose as the Blue Mountains.

The fibro house Whitey sat in sagged at the front. If given the chance, it would one day slide, front bedroom first, into the street it faced. It had been given a coat of baby-blue paint sometime in the seventies, and the panels now looked navy-destroyer grey with sun damage.

Although his housemate had the Housing Commission rental agreement in his name, Peter Crawford, or Pete the Bull, paid no rent himself; for that he let out the front room. Pete lived on cask wine and rollies, and meals prepared mainly by other people. He needed the short-lived, but occasionally warm relationships. And Whitey, a quiet drunk, and always with drugs, had been there for more than four months now.

—Goin' up north next week, Pete said, searching the ashtray for a lightable butt.

—Up north, huh? Whitey replied.

—Yeah. Time ta see the relos I reckon. Even though the cunts come down an' drank all my piss las' month. 'Member?

—Yeah.

Whitey remembered the unpredictability of Pete's brothers and uncles after they'd done their dole on the rum, Coopers and port; and the port on Pete the Bull's niece's lips.

Pete the Bull poured Fruity Lexia into an RSL schooner glass that'd found its way into his possession.

—Want some gooney, Whitey?

—Yeah, fuckit.

Whitey liked the buzz of morning wine, but the afternoons then tended to be down and nauseous; but there was goey today.

Whitey skimmed off the top, but never ripped anyone off. Price and quantity were, in this area of retail, predetermined, well-known, and unquestioned. Credit could be obtained, but terms were very short. On the flipside though, unlike the more commercially established credit organisations, there was nil interest.

The supply of recreational drugs was not an industry that Whitey had exactly chosen as a career. Rather, he'd found himself selling them by default. Before drugs, the teenage Patrick White had found life uninteresting and uncomfortable. He found himself at odds with how his classmates seemed to deal with each other and with life so ardently, but with a kind of effortlessness. Whitey couldn't find anything to really get into the way others did. He liked heavy metal music, but only because there was nothing in pop music he could relate to. The devotion of the metal-heads at his school seemed contrived to him though. And he never really had much to say to anyone. He could sum up everything in a few words when he had to talk, and he was aware that his conversations left others waiting for something more from him that didn't seem to be there, making him feel self-conscious and wanting to talk even less. He got into using drugs not through curiosity, but because it seemed like an easy way to become part of something. And quite instantly, Whitey found people who accepted him and seemed to know how to express humour and indulge in maximum leisure; and best of all at that time, some of these people were female. The notion that drugs were dangerous, as Whitey had heard innumerable times when the cops visited the school to give lectures, seemed ridiculous. Drugs helped, soothed and enhanced life. Drugs were a communal thing. Whitey had something in common, finally.

For all the English, maths and science exams, it was only the extracurricular activities that'd paid off. For Whitey, selling beat the hell out of working for wages. But, like his experiences of working for wages, it wasn't really what he wanted to do. He didn't know what he really wanted to do, but selling seemed to be a transitory occupation. But again, a transition to what, he didn't really know.

Booze World didn't open until ten-thirty in the morning, so the ten am weekdays' airing of the *Jerry Springer Show* was the *Breakfast Show* for most of the inhabitants of the twin Housing Commission estates. On pension day, or at least more noticeably on pension day, people would be standing around the reinforced glass doors waiting for Agro, owner and theft dissuader, to unlock. As well, people would roll up to Pete the Bull's place to score off Whitey by the time the theme credits had flashed on Springer.

Whitey preferred to sell only to those he knew, so if someone was going to be a regular, an introduction had to be made. The worn steps to the house were cracked and buffeted the fibro when stepped on, giving away any approach to the front door. It was early afternoon when Whitey heard someone's tread for the seventeenth time that day. He checked the peephole, spied Natalie Caxaro, an ex-lover of his, and unlocked the door. Natalie and Whitey had had sex with each other exclusively for a time in summer the year before. They'd never really broken up, just stopped having sex; and so didn't see each other much any more.

—Nat. Howsitgoin? Whitey said, and nodded slightly toward the guy who was standing next to her, whom Whitey had not seen through the peephole.

—This is Eddie, she said. I know 'im from the club. He's cool. Whitey let them in.

—What ya after? Whitey asked Nat, but quietly.

—Eddie wants to talk to ya, she said; and gave in to her bladder that had begun to burn since the ride over to Whitey's. Can I use ya dunny?

—Yeah, Whitey said, and sat down. He sipped some wine and looked up at this Eddie guy. Sit down if ya want, mate. Whitey motioned to the torn green chair.

—Tah. So, Nat tells me you may be able to set me up with some decent speed. I'm after an ounce, at least to start with, Eddie said, sitting and gripping his hands together like a Catholic praying.

—An oz? That'd wipe me out, mate, Whitey replied. Best I can do is a couple a eight balls.

—Well, maybe you could put me in touch with your dealer, Eddie suggested, and rubbed both his thighs.

Whitey didn't answer, but scratched his neck and watched Nat walk back into the lounge room. This guy seemed like a bit of a yuppie. His hair was too deliberately tousled, his jeans too newish. Whitey wondered if Nat was trying to make him jealous. Or maybe make Eddie jealous.

—What about H? Eddie asked.

—Ya don't look much like a user ta me, mate, Whitey said.

—Not for me. But I'm after some for some friends of mine.

—I'll see what I can do. I'll let Nat know if I can get hold a some. So, ya after anything smaller than an oz?

—Any chance of getting hold of your dealer to see about the ounce and the H? Eddie asked.

—Nuh.

Whitey held up his glass as Pete the Bull stepped into the lounge room. Pete had a massive torso, but long, thin legs, and moved silently. Through living with the man, Whitey was able to sense his sudden presence — it could be menacing, but it was a comfort in this situation. He knew he wouldn't like the look of this Eddie guy either. Pete poured some gooney into Whitey's glass, and nodded at Nat.

—'O's this cunt then, he said, looking sideways at Eddie.

—The name's Eddie, mate. You're Peter, right?

—Hey, do I know you, cunt?

—No, I —

—Well fuck off. Go on, git.

Whitey looked at Nat and shrugged his shoulders. She motioned to Eddie, and he got up to leave.

—So, let me know about what we talked about, huh? Eddie said to Whitey, who'd ceased to look at him.

—Yeah, he said.

Whitey watched them leave, Eddie talking closely to Nat as they walked quickly to a late-model Ford XR6.

—Don't like that cunt, Pete the Bull said. Think I recognise 'im from some place.

—I think 'is just a rich prick. Some try-hard Nat wants ta bang, Whitey said.

—Tell her ta come on her own next time, Pete said, and sparked the rollie sitting on his lip.

It was a good day, but then pension day always was. Disability and Sickness Benefit recipients received more than Unemployment Benefit clients — their stipend was at least two hundred dollars more a fortnight — and the payment was always put into accounts every second Thursday; unlike the dole, which was paid depending on the day of the week the recipient joined the queue. Of course, not all pensioners scored drugs, but many of them offered short-term loans to their off-week dole friends. It was always a big day for Agro at Booze World and Whitey at 22 Acacia Avenue.

He'd moved two ounces of pot and nearly one of goey. For every ounce of pot he sold he made a hundred bucks. For every oz of goey, about a hundred and twenty dollars, but it varied depending on the uncut price. With this on top of his dole payment, tomorrow night would be one to forget at the Workers Arms Hotel.

Whitey grilled some Homely Brand frozen fish fillets and threw them on a plate next to half a loaf of bread. The bread was showing blue mould, but only on the outer crust. He ate one fillet and bread, but left the rest for Pete. He was pissed and had had three lines of goey. Food just didn't fit the mood.

He sat down in front of the telly to watch Law and Order. But speed made watching television a chore. Waves of elation would make him totally empathise with the cast and plot, but then his attention would slip and he'd become impatient with the insipidity of it. He pulled two cones in a row, as a counterweight. He would have liked to ride the speed and alcohol, to go up the pub, but he had to stay in. Pension night could be bigger than the day; people would be coming back for more drugs, because they'd gluttonised in the fever of payday, while others would be just getting out of bed.

The Workers Arms was in Seven Hills, next to an older Housing Commission estate that'd gone mostly private back in the eighties when the government offered Commission tenants a purchase-cost reduction calculated according to how many years they'd paid rent on the property. It was three stations away on the city train, but you could walk it in about half an hour with a few lines of goey under your belt. The signposts that marked the borders of the suburbs were simply nomenclature anyway. The large, sparse blocks of land that sat like static moats around flat houses blended yellow and grey-green into each other. The surviving ghost gums and stringybarks rose and reached out and collectively marked the distinction between the interchangeable outer suburbs and the deciduous inner-urban environment.

The pub hadn't been refurbished in quite a few decades, unlike the majority of its competition who'd gone Irish or cosmopolitan, and that was why it packed out on Fridays and Saturdays. The beer was cheap, the bouncers lenient, and the décor unpretentious. Union banners and prize catches from the fishing club, and red carpet that soaked up whatever was thrown at it. AC/DC shot holes in conversation, firing from the old jukie speakers. But then

Bon Scott spoke for just about everyone in the room anyway; as Angus and Malcolm's Marshalled riffs perfectly complemented the nicotine-stained air they vibrated through.

Whitey hadn't slept the night before and had felt like shit all day. But now, eleven schooners later, the smoky air tasted good, the music filled his chest, and everything could be laughed at.

—Patrick White. You look fuckable tonight. Got any goey?

It was Nat. She was pissed; an all-dayer it looked like to Whitey.

—Nah, he said. You know I don't carry drugs in here since the pigs fucked everything up.

But he was lying. He did have a couple of lines, but only for personal use.

—Buy me a bourbon, Nat said.

—In a minute. Here, have a sip of me beer.

She drained off half the schooner. Her eyes had lost focus ability, but a fierceness had replaced it. He'd never seen her this drunk. Somewhere in the back of his own bender, he wondered what had got her to this. He would have maybe asked, but she changed his thoughts suddenly.

—We should fuck tonight, she said.

—Oh yeah? And why's that, Caxaro?

—*Just because*, White.

There was always a queue to get drinks on a Friday night; it paid to get as many as you could carry whenever you were up there. Whitey ordered three schooners and three bourbon and cokes.

—Thanks, babe, Nat said.

Her drunk's confidence was beginning to be a turn-on for Whitey.

—No wukkas. Drink up.

—So, any chance of getting a line a goey if I come back ta yours? she asked.

—That could be a possibility. You never know your luck in the Greater West, Whitey said. We'll finish these and get something takeaway for the trip home.

Nat skulled a bourbon and attempted to tongue-kiss Whitey, getting as much cheek as mouth.

On the train, Nat pushed Whitey down on the three-seater and lay on top of him. He enjoyed her aggression. They tongue-kissed and drank straight bourbon.

—So who was Mr Aftershave the other day? Whitey asked.

Nat sat up.

—Eddie, she said, looking at the bourbon bottle.

—Yeah. Who's he?

—I told ya. I know 'im from the club. Wests.

—Bit of a yuppie isn't he?

—Yeah. Don't worry 'bout 'im. If we're lucky neither of us'll ever see 'im again. He's fuckin' weird. Acts one way, then another. I dunno, forget him.

—Yeah well, Pete don't want him 'round at the house again, so if he wants ta score, you'll have ta come on ya Pat Malone, Whitey said, taking a slug from the bottle.

—Mmm, she said.

In his bedroom, Whitey put Metallica's ... And *Justice for All* on the CD player, lined up two thin caterpillars of speed and passed the mirror to Nat. She did the line, but nearly wasted the second one with a clumsy breath. Whitey finger-licked the remaining line and let the sweet/savoury/acidic goodness slug its way down his throat. They got into his bed and Whitey dragged off her jeans and panties. He kissed her vagina, but it didn't seem like his kisses were doing much. He moved up to her head.

—Nat?

But she snored and rolled away.

Fuckin' waste of goey, Whitey thought. He plugged his headphones into the CD player and picked up the bottle of bourbon.

When he came-to the next morning, Nat was gone. Whitey hadn't heard her leave. The bourbon bottle was tipped over, but there was no spillage; its contents had been spilled unremembered down his throat. He did vaguely remember some air-drumming to 'Eye of the Beholder' though. His room looked grey, like the hard, lonely hangover that was waiting to strike — or rather, constrict.

In the lounge room Pete sat with a glass of pale wine rolling White Ox into thin cigarettes.

—Get lucky, ya bastard? Pete said.

—Not exactly.

—She woke me up tryin' ta open the door, Pete moaned, spitting a piece of tobacco.

—Dodgin' a mornin' glory as well as last night, Whitey said.

—Glass a gooney, mate?

—Nah. I gotta eat somethin'. Hungry?

—If ya makin'.

Whitey threw two Black Ben pies in the oven for Pete and stir-fried some frozen vegetables for himself. He tried the bread, but mould had won over a new colony. He drank straight from the tap until his stomach rejected. He groaned. He had to ring Ronnie, his drug supplier, and exchange some cash for stash, but the idea filled him with despair. Maybe after food ideas would feel better. He ate despite the tastelessness.

—I dunno how ya do it, Whitey said, putting the two pies down on the scarred coffee table.

—Do what?

—Not suffer from hangovers.

—I get 'em. *Just* don' fuckin' whinge, Pete replied.

—Well, I'm off it for a while, Whitey said.

—Fuckin' have a glass a gooney, ya weak white cunt, Pete laughed.

So Whitey had some wine and Whitey arranged to get some more drugs the next day. And later, Pete packed some clothes and a gooney bladder in a once-blue sports bag for his trip up north.

Dogs.

—Every dog has its day, the guy with dog-ears said. Bark — Bark.

The guy climbed through the ceiling, and Whitey moved closer to consciousness because, as he'd begun to suspect, he was in a dream. He awoke to hear the tail-end of one of his snores. Every dog in the street was going off. Whitey rolled over and looked at the digital clock on the floor next to his bed. Five forty-three am. He rolled back over. It was Tuesday. There was no reason to get up this early on a Tuesday. He closed his eyes, but the dogs continued. He heard the side-gate move. He got up, looked out the window. It was dream-like, but: dogs, white cars, vans. Cops. Fuck. Ronnie'd dropped off a shit-load on Sunday. He pulled on his jeans.

Should he hide the drugs? Or himself?

Or vomit the speedy bile?

The front door was belted out of the door-frame. Whitey stuck his head around the bedroom doorway. Eddie was there, in the lounge room, now with cuffs and a gun on his belt. Whitey was slammed to the floor. A knee was on his cheek and another in his back. They were going through everything. With the dogs. The television. Broken drawers. The knee now on his jaw. There'd been drugs everywhere in here. The dogs were too efficient. Too professional. Black, small. Labrador. Maybe too small for a labrador. They were finding rewards. The knee on his jaw shifted, the weight transferred fully to his back.

The pigs — and their dogs — could take all liberties.

Whitey slid the dry, plastic-skinned sausage and the poached egg into the toilet bowl, but they didn't flush. The purgatory of the Bellevue Remand Centre was holding off severe turbulence — for both semi-processed meats and criminals it seemed. The ecru paint was thick on the walls. You could feel the below-ground level coldness in them, but for Whitey, it was not enough to make them real. Like the feeling in his head. He was numb but somehow sharply aware. He'd not felt this helpless, stripped and disabled since he was a kid, and his father had been taken from him. And like then, he could do nothing but let it happen — to live the experience from as much distance as his mind would allow. He didn't want to think too far ahead either. As much as he was hating the situation, he knew it could get worse. There was that threat everywhere. On the faces of his fellow detainees. In the hardness of the limited amenities.

And that night, after a full day in remand, Whitey lay on the mat they gave him for a bed and wondered how his luck had gone so bad. He didn't want much out of his life. But one thing was clear now. What he did want was freedom. And that was thinning out. He wondered if his own carelessness had brought on this bad luck. Of course Eddie was a cop. The thought hadn't really entered his mind then, but why would Nat bring someone over out of the blue? She never had before. He should have just told them both to fuck off. But he wouldn't. He'd never told anyone to fuck off when they'd come to buy drugs. It was just plain fucking bad luck. And anyway, it was out of his control now.

TWO

Sonja Marmeladova looked out the window of her Year 10 English class at the dogs humping on the oval. She liked English, it was her favourite subject, but today she was over Othello. The dogs were real, living their poetry. The bitch broke from the male and went back to sniffing and eating recess scraps.

—So. Is Othello a hero or a villain? Miss de Groen asked the class.

But still Sonja couldn't be bothered. She looked back out the window. To the dogs and their simple happiness.

When the bell went, Sonja headed for the library. As much as she wanted to learn more about and embrace Australian culture, lately she liked to read Russian novels. Dostoyevsky's nineteenth-century St Petersburg was not exactly the Moscow she had left only half a decade ago, but she could live it in her head. The author's words, in translation, were difficult, but there'd be sentences that would grab some inner part of her, and bring back scents, and the unharsh light of her earlier childhood. She'd finished the large book, and although not entirely grasped it, got something from it she wanted to live again.

She took Chekhov's Plays off the shelf and read the introduction. She borrowed it when the bell rang, then headed for her history class.

—Hey, Sonja, howsitgoin'?

It was Raz, a Year 11 boy. She'd sat with his group once or twice at lunch — or found herself sitting in their hangout by mistake — and had had some decent conversations. But she couldn't remember actually talking to Raz in particular.

—Good, she replied.

—I was lookin' for ya t'day, Raz said.

—Me. Why?

—I just wanted ta ask ya somehin'.

—Well, here I am, she said.

—I'll find ya t'morrow, okay? I, um, gotta get ta class, Raz said, and motioned up the hall, to his next class Sonja supposed.

—Okay.

It was hard to focus on history. Raz. He was pretty good-looking. Not that she'd ever really thought about him in that way. His friend Brett had sex-appeal, and she'd thought about him. But Raz ... She put Chekhov on her lap and began The Cherry Orchard under the desk, to take her mind off Raz. What could he want? From her?

Sonja picked up her younger sister, Polly, from the primary school on her way home. Today, Polly's hair looked like a forgotten doll's: Sonja hadn't had time to brush it before school, and there would be a tug-o-war tonight to cure the knots.

—Do you think we'll have pancakes for dinner tonight? Polly asked.

—If Dad brings home some milk, I told you, Sonja replied patiently, not for the first time.

But she wasn't hungry now. Raz. She hated hope. Or at least the emptiness that usually followed hope. She couldn't help hoping Raz liked her though. It was such a sudden feeling. It was something she'd never wished for before: a guy liking her. But its implications were massive. It would mean someone thought of her as pretty. It would mean that her Russianness was not an abnormality. It would mean she was part of someone, who was part of something.

She grabbed Polly's hand as they dared the highway — a little further east than usual, as the linesmen working on the overhead power lines that framed the highway had spread orange witches hats over what seemed like an excessive area of the highway shoulder.

Sonja lived with her parents and her younger sister and brother in a small two-bedroom flat in Brunei Court, the Housing Commission complex in Mt Druitt. The three children shared one bedroom, and there was one more that their parents shared — except when the father, Zakhar, was drinking. Then there was the combined lounge room/kitchenette, and a bathroom-cum-laundry. They'd all lived with the mother's cousin for the first two years in Australia, but the father had pissed on the lounge and spilled his wine too many times. They no longer spoke to Katerina's cousin. After a few weeks in the hostel, the Commission had offered her family the unit in Brunei Court. It was only meant to be temporary, but after Zakhar had apparently severely insulted Commission staff, their place on the waiting list for a larger house had slipped.

Zakhar Marmeladov had been an academic. He'd taught mathematics in Moscow and worked as a civil engineer. And as far as Sonja could remember, her father had not wanted to migrate to Australia. Sonja's auntie had written to them of the liberty, the shared wealth, and the healthy dry heat of Australia. Katerina Marmeladova had decided they would make the seemingly endless and certainly uncomfortable journey south, and south. It had been her dream, she always told them after vodka, to live and educate her children abroad. Katerina was a voracious reader of anything from the West, and her aspirations had flourished since Yeltsin. Zakhar, Sonja remembered, relented when he was transferred to the army — something he'd avoided obstinately — to teach engineering. In his stubbornness the tickets were bought and her mother expedited their visa application.

The ride from the airport to her auntie's place in the south-west corner of the suburban spread had been so contrary to what Sonja had been looking forward to. She had had to ask if they were in Sydney, or was there another leg of the trip to be taken? It was all trees and grass and highway, and flat, sterile buildings hiding low amongst the growth. And the greens, yellows and greys were like nothing she had ever imagined. They were almost a single colour. The shapes of the trees were so un-conforming, so like naked human limbs. And then her auntie's house. Her auntie apologised that they'd all have to be squashed. But there was enough space for another family as far as Sonja could tell. And it was quiet. The days were eerie. Sonja would listen for cars, for voices in the street. They barely came.

The excursions, finally, into the city were something though. How super-new it looked with its sharp, angled glass buildings compared to Moscow. Her father disliked it. He criticised the architecture, the endless rows of shops, the pompous cafés. He was right, Sonja thought. But it was nicer than the necropolis of her auntie's suburb, Leumeah.

Their immigration visa was granted. Her father's status as an engineer had ensured it. She heard him cursing his degrees the day the letter came. Zakhar had begun working for a builder — a Russian friend of Sonja's auntie. From his first day he had complained about the builder. He'd lived too long in this every-day-is-Christmas wonderland, he said. He's interested only in profit, profit, and substandard offerings.

Zakhar had always been a drinker. Her uncles, her aunties, her cousins, her friends' parents had always drunk. But here, in the silent suburb, her father began to detach from them, and to celebrate his un-fulfilment and regret daily, and nightly, with vodka and beer.

—Beer, this piss, they love their fucking beer here, she heard him murmuring through his beer alone in the lounge room one night.

Soon her father was no longer working for the builder. And towards the end of their stay at her auntie's, she heard her auntie say that Zakhar had lost the job because he'd been drinking at work, and had stored bottles and bottles of urine under his desk.

The move to Brunei Court was liberating. The flat made you aware that you were part of a family. Sonja could hear her siblings and parents from every room. And although it was just as far west of the city as her auntie's was south-west, the noise of the highway behind the flats was constant comfort. It was proof of life. She'd had to change schools, but she'd wanted a second go at that anyway. The first school she'd attended had taught her little academically. There was too much social nuance to take in. The kids had freedom to learn, in a variety of methods, or not to learn at all if they chose. And instead of the straight stick, the straight back, and the straight mouth, kids could slouch and giggle. There was even time to lie on the carpeted floor and read! Sonja could understand the English they spoke here, but articulating it was an exhaustive process. She'd learned it was better to not say much. Teachers rewarded this as much as correct answers.

But at her new school Sonja decided she would learn more of what her teachers could offer her, and less about what her fellow students demonstrated. Though that, of course, proved impossible. There was always something revealed to her. These kids knew so much about sex. They were having sex. They had relationships. There were whole class-times behind the teachers' backs devoted to the dramas of these relationships. Sonja had not attended high school in Moscow, but she could not imagine this happening in a Russian high school. At least not so publicly. The kids asked her if she had a boyfriend. If she had a girlfriend. The girls asked her who she liked. She didn't know. They were all so foreign. They looked okay. But they acted like the characters she saw on the television. So wondered if they were real. Or would she become an actor too if she was taken into a relationship? Of course there was always the classes and books to distract her, luckily.

Her father didn't work even after they'd moved into the flat. They were able to get a payment from the government each fortnight — marked by three days of increasingly predictable mood swings from her parents. The payment day would be a celebration. They would have roasted pork, potatoes and sour cream, and bread rolls. There would be vodka. Then beer. Then wine. Then horrible sweet-smelling wine from a box. And her father's mood would sour. Her mother would also come down from the feast day. Sharply reminding them all that if Zakhar would embrace Australia, every day could be feast day. Sonja could see that her father was searching for the celebration again in the days of continued drinking. But it revealed how he saw his life in Australia. As a waste.

On a bright summer night, at the tail-end of a bender, Zakhar was run over near their home. His liver and stomach, having been belted far up into his chest cavity, had stopped his breathing. Some other tenants of Brunei Court who were just beginning their bender had heard the thump of his body hitting the asphalt and had gone out onto the highway to protect him from being further ruined by the onslaught of traffic. Zakhar survived and his repaired diaphragm eventually healed enough for the liver infection to set in. He'd become sick so quickly that Sonja was sure the nurse had mixed up her patients when she was telling them the news. Sonja, even after the accident, hadn't really considered that her father would die in Australia. She prayed to God that he at least would get to see Russia again. And when he was able to communicate again, she would never forget what he told her of what he'd dreamed, or experienced, while in the induced coma. Of the vastness, the immenseness of the universe. And, helpless, being helped, carried back; a subconscious consciousness had been turned back on and his life force had reclaimed his intubated body. And how he wasn't scared to die anymore. But didn't want to drink.

Six weeks later, the Welfare Centre sent him to the job at the tallow factory where he worked on the bottling line that forced out detergents under high pressure. The family had been eating, and he hadn't been drinking. But one night Sonja heard him say the first Australianism she'd ever heard from him: the job was enough to drive a man to drink.

It was before rollcall and some of the girls were in the toilets still deciding whether or not to wag. Sonja regarded herself in the cracked and graffitied mirror. The girls next to her looked at themselves with confidence. They knew boys would be watching them, wanting them — they'd be turning boys down. Sonja wasn't sure whether she was attractive or not. Sometimes at home, alone in front of the bathroom mirror, she thought she looked pretty. But here, alongside the other girls, she thought she looked weird — short, slight, but maybe a little older than them. She had the features of a woman, she'd been told. It was possible that Raz liked her look; she liked guys who had their own original look.

Sitting in class, Sonja tried to picture Raz in her head. But she couldn't. It wasn't that she didn't know what he looked like — it was the opposite. She'd been thinking about him, looking for him, all morning. But the exact lines of his face wouldn't come — like looking at a picture too closely. She hated how she was thinking now. How such a small and stupid thing — a boy noticing her — could consume so much of her energy. She couldn't focus on maths: it was droning on like it never had before, even though she'd had a long toilet break. She wished she knew what class Raz was in now. She kept picturing him in the science labs, but that was probably because she'd just come from science. She tried to read The Cherry Orchard again under her desk. But Chekhov's words were just too subtle compared to what was going on in her head. Eventually, the lunch bell rang.

Sonja wandered around the quadrangle, trying to look casual. Raz was nowhere to be seen. She spotted his friend Brett, and kept him in eyeshot. But no Raz. Then she saw him. Or was it him? Yes. But suddenly, she wished it wasn't him. He saw her and headed over. Shit, she thought.

—Hey, Sonja, Raz said. And he did look kind of different from what she'd remembered. He seemed younger. And his mouth. It was cute. He really had no top lip. But it gave his mouth a childlike look she hadn't noticed the day before.

—Hello, she answered, as casual as possible.

—How ya goin'? Raz said, and finished the mandarin he was eating.

—I'm good. You?

—Good. Good.

—So, um, do you live in Mt Druitt?

—Yes. Yes, I do. You too? she said.

—Nuh, in Rooty Hill, but I've seen ya 'round Brunei Court. I go there ta see a mate sometimes. Well, anyway, I was thinkin' maybe we could hang out a bit, after school an' that 'ay, if ya wanted to.

—Okay, that sounds pretty cool. What would we do? she said.

—I dunno, just hang out, we live pretty close an' that, we could just hang out, talk an' that, he said, and scratched his leg.

—Okay, what, today? she said. Unless you're doing something else, she quickly added.

—Nuh, today sounds cool. What about at the Lebo shop, I mean, the takeaway on Vivisector Street, ya know it?

—Yes. I think I know the shop. So, what time?

—I dunno, half past four, five-ish? he said.

—Okay, I'll see you there, Sonja replied, and smiled, and she could tell he liked it.

She picked up Polly from the primary school and kissed her on the head.

—What was that for? Polly asked.

—Because you're so cute.

—Thank you, Soney, Polly said, and kissed her sister's hand. Will we have pancakes for dinner tonight?

—Yes. Yes, I think we will, Sonja answered.

And they crossed the highway, again having to detour around the linesmen's witches hats. Sonja smiled at the guy strapping on his safety harness.

Today Brunei Court didn't look so bad. The sun shining off the broken glass in the carpark had lost its piercing glare: today it was more of a brilliant highlight in the asphalt's rich texture. The sounds of domestic disharmony bouncing out of the stairwells had lost their insidious edge. Until she recognised one of the raised voices as her mother's.

Sonja's father had never hit any of his family. He'd shoved his wife when she'd tried to confiscate alcohol, but violence for its own sake was never the motive. Katerina Marmeladova also enjoyed a drink. But she soon found herself doing anything to discourage Zakhar from drinking. Because now Zakhar, once started, would continue until something of himself, and those around him, had been drunk off. His keeping a job kept the family part of their adopted community; and fuelled the hope for more as long as he prevailed. But alcohol quickly became his nebula. He needed to be at the centre of it, and its gases affected them all. In Russia, Zakhar had held the power in the Marmeladov family. Now, Katerina would yell at Zakhar until he left the house or ceased drinking. Either way, they knew it would mean a day off work.

Today she was yelling at her husband, in Russian, and in a dialect that Sonja found harsh and hard to understand, and in English, because it unsettled him. But although Zakhar grimaced, he continued to draw moselle from the cask he'd brought home. He sat on the floor, with his back against the lounge.

—Prkola, he said. It was his drunk curse word. Sonja didn't know exactly what it meant, and had never asked. She doubted its Russianness.

—Are you okay, Ma? she asked.

—Sonja. Please. Look at your father. No, don't. And don't talk to him, Katerina hissed. Her mother's eyes changed when she got into this mood. They reminded Sonja of a husky's eyes — they'd go a wild blue. But also they wouldn't focus, they'd dart around you, and her eyelids would flutter as if she was about to scream. And her mother would perpetually push her hair back behind her ears.

—Where's Peter? Sonja asked, looking at some scribbly drawings her brother had done on the back of a cardboard box.

—He's in the room. He's scared of his own father. Scared, Sonja. Of his own father.

Katerina yelled at her husband again in the dialect reserved for his drunkenness.

Sonja took Polly's hand and went in to her brother. Peter had been crying, but he'd found a game to play with his makeshift toys and had forgotten why the tears had cleaned a path down his cheeks. Sonja hugged him. She looked up at Polly. Pancakes were doubtful. Any meal was doubtful. Unless Sonja cooked something. Katerina Marmeladova indulged in emotions as her husband indulged in thick oblivion. The parents were wasted tonight.

Sonja went back out into the hot, thick air.

—Are you okay, Dad? Are you feeling sick? she asked.

—Sonja. My beautiful daughter.

Zakhar had spilled wine down his shirt and on his crotch. He looked too pathetic to hate. Besides, Sonja knew he thought he was only abusing himself. It was a different story with her mother though. Her reaction to his drinking was becoming a habit, and a predictable one. Sonja wondered whether her mother thought it was the right thing to do to yell and cry and nag her husband and neglect everything else. The thing was, though, that her mother wasn't like this when her father was sober; the situation was his fault.

Sonja made some toast with stale dark rye bread. There was no butter, of course, so she drizzled some vegetable oil over it. The three children ate; the mother sat and cursed, occasionally yelling; and the father sat and drank, eventually wetting himself on the lounge-room floor.

Sonja and Polly slept together in the single bed. Peter slept in the broken, paint-peeled cot behind the door. Sonja hugged her sister and smelt her hair. She loved it. It was her home smell. Lying back down away from her sister's perfect little head, Sonja began to think of Raz. Shit, Raz. She'd pushed it to the back of her mind when she'd seen her father's — and her mother's — state. Shit. She hoped he wouldn't be too pissed off, that he'd still want to meet her another time. But she didn't want to think about it too much, because he probably would be pissed off, and wouldn't even want to talk to her again. She'd have to think of an excuse; one that wouldn't make her family look neurotic and alcoholic — one that seemed normal and Aussie.

Once, last year, in Year 9, a boy had brought a magazine to school. He was showing all the girls the pictures in it and laughing at them when they said yuck. Sonja had looked at the pictures. A woman had a man's penis in her mouth. He also had it in her down there, and in her bum-hole. In one of the pictures, the man was holding his penis and it was spurting pearly liquid onto the woman's stomach. She said yuck as well, but later, at home that night, she wished she could look at the pictures again.

Nothing like that could happen to her, she was sure. It was nothing she'd ever experience. The boys at school were just that: boys. The people in the pictures, especially the men, seemed very adult. Veiny, muscular, confident. The pictures had been strangely arousing, but they were alien, of another breed. Any attraction she had to the boys at school, like Raz, was more about wanting them to find her appealing. Sex with these boys seemed way too remote. She doubted they looked anything like, or could do anything like, the men in those pictures.

Sonja was pissed off with her parents. For making it a miserable night again — the first of many to come if she knew her father. And for making it impossible to meet up with Raz. But the night had made her feel differently about the whole Raz thing. The curiosity had fermented overnight, and now she just wanted to know why he wanted to hang out with her.

She finished urinating and washed her hands in the stained stainless-steel washbasin. She looked in the quarter of mirror above the basin. Today, at least, she just didn't care. The rollcall bell rang and she left the smoky, cheap-perfumey toilets.

Raz was outside the toilet block, spitting and kicking pebbles.

—Hey, Sonja, he said.

—Hey.

—Did you forget about yesterday? he asked, lightly kicking the ground.

—No. Look, I'm so sorry. I had a family thing that came up suddenly. I should have got your phone number, I'm sorry, really, Raz.

—That's okay, I thought maybe I scared you off, he said, but not with the confidence the statement should carry.

—No. I wasn't scared. I was kind of looking forward to it, actually, Sonja said.

—Yeah? Raz squinted a smile at Sonja. What class ya got now?

—Maths.

—I got commerce. I'm thinkin' of waggin' but, Raz said.

—What are you going to do then?

—Dunno. Maybe go down Brownthistle Park, hang out for a bit.

—Oh, Sonja said. She wasn't sure if Brownthistle sounded any more exciting than maths class, but being with Raz was certainly more enticing. It was a strange request, but then everything here seemed a bit strange. And girls did seem to suddenly get boyfriends within the space of a class. This could quite likely be how it happened. Mind if I come?

—'Course not. I was hoping you would.

Brownthistle Park lay in a gully between Rooty Hill and Mt Druitt. There was the skeleton of a children's adventure playground, and an open stormwater drain running through it. There was also an amenities shed, burnt-out, but still squatting firmly on its foundations.

Raz and Sonja sat on the slat bench outside the shed. The black and grey bricks and the blue sky above made it seem like this was a real experience, like she was doing something that would awaken her to the Aussie way of life. She was glad she'd ditched maths.

—I like your hair, Raz said, and touched it with sweaty fingers.

—Thank you, she replied. But it was a compliment she'd never expected.

Raz took out a packet of Stradbroke Blues and offered Sonja one.

—No thanks. I don't smoke. Thanks though, she said.

He lit one and touched her thigh. Sonja thought she felt a tremble in his touch, but then, it could have been her.

—I like your legs.

—Thanks, she said and looked at him. She liked it, and would kiss him if he got rid of the cigarette.

Raz blew out blue smoke and leant in to kiss Sonja. Their front teeth clashed, but so did their lips. Sonja kissed back. She'd never kissed before. She moved in closer to him. His body made her feel like getting closer. It wasn't like the feeling she got from those pictures she saw last year; she wanted to feel, not see. She wanted to be too close to see. Raz tossed the cigarette and pulled Sonja onto his lap, facing him. They kissed. She rubbed her vagina on him. It was too much. The kissing, the being inside each other's mouths. Raz touched the top of her thighs, under her panties. He tried to pull them off, but it was impossible in this position.

—Stand up, he said.

She stood. She was dizzy, but smiled at him. He moved her up against the shed wall and pulled down her panties. They kissed. Raz lifted up Sonja's school skirt and looked at her. He whispered something she didn't catch and undid his school trousers and dropped his undies. He held his penis. Sonja looked at it. It was like a junior version of the one in the pictures — she suddenly remembered a junior scale guitar a friend of hers had had back in Russia. He held it up to her vagina and rubbed it on her lips. She opened her legs slightly. Raz groaned and her vagina lips felt warm and something tickled the inside of her thigh.

—Aah. Shit. Fuck. Did you come? he asked.

—Um. I don't know? she said.

—I thought you were coming too.

Sonja didn't answer. She looked at the semen running over her knee. She would've liked to have kissed and touched some more, but the sudden coldness of the semen told her it was over. She pulled up her panties as Raz had already done up his pants and grabbed his bag.

—Listen, I gotta go, he said.

Surprisingly, there was toilet paper in the shed. Sonja wiped herself clean and walked out of the park. It was way too early to pick up Polly, so she headed home.

She felt like she was observing herself and her surroundings through a milky, amnesic filter. It didn't make them look any better. The carpark annexed by Brunei Court seemed unforgiving — sunburned, tired, and in need of sympathy itself; the broken glass sharp and aggressive. And she saw her father sitting on the first step of their stairwell. By his side was a cask of white burgundy.

—Sonja. Your mother kicked me out. Kicked me out of my own home, Zakhar Marmeladov said, shifting the cask behind his leg.

—Didn't you go to work today? Sonja asked, and walked past him.

—I was sick today, he called back to her, but she was already at the front door.

Sonja walked through the flat, ignoring her mother, and lay face down on the bed. What the hell was that? Was she Raz's girlfriend now? She doubted it. He seemed to quite suddenly regret being with her and getting so excited. He'd come — what he'd called it — like the guy in those pictures. Why had he just left like that? Had she made him do it the wrong way? She knew though, watching his back as he walked away, that that was probably it. She wouldn't be Raz's girlfriend.

THREE

Senior Sergeant Salvatore Testafiglia pulled into his double driveway and pressed the horn of his assigned deep-blue late model Commodore. Maria, his wife, was meant to have the garage door open by the time he arrived home, but today she'd neglected to. Maria, reacting to the two controlled but urgent horn blows came out of the double ornamental front doors and ran to the garage door. She looked through the windshield to gauge his mood, and slid open the aluminum shutter.

Everything about the house was double. Double storey, double garage, double brick. Salvatore's cousin, Melito, had built it. The house was in Newington, a suburb on the Parramatta River that had been advantaged by the Sydney Olympic development and the demolition of warehousing and industry. The petrolly mud on the banks of the Parramatta River had become a valuable commodity. The Testafiglias had moved out of the Italian precinct of inner-city Leichhardt when Salvatore had been posted out to the Western Plateau Local Patrol three years earlier. He'd crowned the house with a short sandstone wall so the family could watch the fireworks from the flat roof on New Year's Eve.

Inside the leather and tile house, the family lived in the large kitchen. The formal lounge was off-limits, except to dust, polish and vacuum. The formal dining room was strictly for the favoured Aunt and Uncle, and the upstairs was for sleeping. Along with his wife, Salvatore kept two children in the house. Charlie was sixteen, and Artemesia, his daughter, was seventeen. He and Maria had tried for more children, only to be shamed by Salvatore's sister's unpaused fecundity. Salvatore had only recently ceased the constant attempts at increasing his heirs, mainly due to the embarrassment he suffered when the doctor told him that he had to give Maria a break so her bladder infections would clear up.

But despite the smallness of his family, Salvatore's existence was what was expected.

And he expected things in his house to similarly conform to his wishes.

—Where's Mia? Salvatore asked as he sat down to the pasta lenticia.

—She, ah, rang earlier. She's at a friend's place for dinner, Maria said, cutting the bread.

Charlie stifled a laugh.

—Ai. What's so funny, mister? Salvatore fixed his son with a sharp look, and then addressed Maria. And do you know this friend?

—I think Mia has had her over before, Deba is her name.

—And the parents. Do you know them?

—We haven't met them, but —

—Have you got the address? Salvatore demanded, mixing the pasta with his accusing fork.

—No. But I can ring her on her mobile and —

—After dinner I'll pick her up. Dinner is a family time. Mia knows that.

★

So Salvatore re-dressed in his uniform when he went to pick up Artemesia, because she claimed, when her mother rang her on her mobile phone, that she'd already left her friend's place, and would meet her father at the train station. The uniform would demonstrate not only to Mia, but to anyone stupid enough to be hanging around, that he meant business.

—Where is your friend? he asked his daughter before she could get into the car.

—What do you mean, Daddy? Mia said, kissing his cheek.

—Why didn't she walk you to the station and wait with you? It's dangerous for a young woman, Mia, I know only too well.

—What, and it's only dangerous for me, but not for my friends? she scoffed, drawing back her long, thick dark hair.

—Don't be smart, Mia, you know what I mean, he said. And this is a girlfriend is it?

—Daddy.

—You know I don't want you to have a boyfriend. Not until you're twenty. School and family are what's important now. There'll be plenty of time for boys.

—But, Daddy, Mum said I could have a boyfriend when I'm eighteen.

—Your mother doesn't make the rules.

—Anyway, you're my boyfriend, Daddy.

When they got home Mia went straight to her room. She had everything she needed there: DVD player, stereo, telephone, floor-to-ceiling mirror, hair-straightener, double bed, and a wardrobe fit to burst.

Her brother, Charlie, knocked lightly on her door and opened it slightly.

—Mum told me to bring you up some pasta, Charlie said.

—Thanks, babe. Just put it on the dresser, Mia said, pulling off her stretch Lees.

—So. Were you with him tonight? Charlie asked.

—Sssshhh, she said, and shut the door.

—Well? He leant against the back of the door.

—Yes.

—Ah, Charlie said, blowing his sister a mock kiss.

—Shut up. He wants to meet you. I told him how you like those cars, XYZs or whatever, she said, sitting on the bed, where she could look at herself in the mirror.

—WRXs.

—Like I said, whatever. Anyway, next time we hang, he said to bring you alo– Shit, Dad.

Salvatore knocked on the door.

Charlie left, managing to avoid eye contact.

Senior Sergeant Testafiglia kept a photograph of his family on his desk. It was from several years ago, and Mia still looked like a girl-child. It was a good time. It was a family time. Artemesia loved and, more importantly, respected him then. Now she seemed only to respect people outside the family. Friends and, despite the pain it brought him to think about it, boys, he suspected. She swore she wasn't seeing any boys, but Salvatore knew liars, and there was something of that in his daughter lately. And it all started around the time he suddenly noticed that little Mia was actually a woman. A woman who would be causing lust. And lusting herself. He'd had to start being sterner about what he expected of her. And witness the growing contempt on her face.

But he'd decided not to think about this at work.

There'd been a new development in the community. Most of the crimes in his local patrol were related to domestic violence and drugs and alcohol. Issues that Senior Sergeant Testafiglia felt could be resolved and even annihilated by adhering to simple European family values. However, there had been a second report of a much more brutal and deliberately malicious incident.

Senior Sergeant Testafiglia prepared to give the day-shift a truncated briefing of the events, as was required.

—In both reports, he said, then paused to halt any further talking but his own. In both reports teenage girls have been coaxed into going with a group of eighteen to twenty-year-old boys to smoke marijuana and have then been raped by up to five males. Both girls were Anglo-Saxon, and both had been insulted for their backgrounds by their attackers, who have been described as Middle Eastern and/or Mediterranean, and refer to themselves as a gang. This most likely means they're not from the immediate community. You can pick up descriptions of the guys we're looking for from Clare in Communications. Any further reports of similar incidents are to be forwarded directly to me.

Salvatore rubbed his chin and walked back to his office. Now a taskforce would have to be set up, and that would mean more time away from his family. His daughter. If parents were stricter about their children's whereabouts … At lunchtime he would drive by the school and make sure his daughter was there. He had started doing this every day. As far as he knew, she hadn't noticed him.

PART TWO

FOUR

Condiments were stuck to the stainless-steel tray with sugary glue. Whitey'd never seen anyone use the jars, but they were half full. Breakfast was the same every day — planks of toast, a choice of two cereals, a poached egg — if you wanted it. Lunch and dinner were determined by a roster. Today, Wednesday, was sausage rolls and dogs' eyes for lunch. It was something to look forward to, although before his stretch, which he was six months into, he hadn't gone much for the heavily salted pastries.

He'd worked, for a while, in the workshops, preparing aluminium signs for spraying. But working simply galvanised depression — the way it had outside. So he opted out. Did the exercise, ate, smoked, thought, and pushed down the realisation that time is a natural resource that men have built structures around to process — extricating it in the crudest form. Time had meant little to Whitey on the outside. It flowed with him out there. In here, you were made to feel it. A little more drawn out of you each day. Like a serrated blade being removed, an hour at a time. Well, that was when it was at its worst.

Every second morning they tried to get a man's smell out of the rooms with disinfectant. But the men sweated and farted and shat and pissed and breathed. And came. And so, collectively, let the disinfectant in, but never let it win. This was a world of armpits, purple testi-sacs, and hairy toes with thick, tough nails.

—Hey, Whitey, ya lucky cunt. Gettin' out tamorra? Keithy said.
　—Wha?
　—Saw ya name on the out-board.
　—Fuck off, he said, to buy a moment to get his mind around it, trying to work out if it was a joke.
　—Ah well, fuck ya then, cunt. I don' give a fuck if ya in or out.
　Whitey had misread Keithy's intention.
　So he looked at his name, like it was someone else's, because it was, or it was his but anyone could use it in any way they pleased. His name had been directed to see about the requirements of the Parole Board.

—And what about accommodation? she asked.
　She had a plump face that to Whitey suggested compassion. But then the laugh-lines suggested fakeness.
　—Well, I dunno. I can stay at a mate's place, I s'pose, he said. Whitey had gotten in touch with Pete the Bull through the Prison Community Liaison Office — they'd tracked him down in Townsville — and told him about the bust. With no one living in the house, Pete had had to forfeit the lease.
　—Will that be permanent? asked the clerk, knowing it wouldn't be, but hoping still that he would say yes anyway.
　—Um, I dunno. Probly not. Depends on me mate's missus.

—We can get you emergency accommodation, in public housing. It may take a week or two.

—Yeah, okay, he said.

He'd never had his own place. The thought gave birth to the realisation of his impending freedom. Until she said:

—What area? You can give two preferences. No guarantee, of course. And she turned the monitor to his face, as though he would understand its expression of lines and broken language.

He made a phone call. Ronnie was drunk, but he said that it would be cool with his woman, Michelle, if he stayed a few days. He would organise a party.

On the outside, on a grey day, he looked at this large, careless prison, the world outside jail. He could catch the bus or take a cab from the jail, but he had put on some weight inside and his clothes, folded for too long, felt like they needed the movement, so he walked.

He thought about the lesson he'd learned. He didn't want to go back inside again. In many ways, it wasn't as bad as he'd imagined. There was no forced anal sex. He didn't get bashed. In fact, he'd learnt that, just like outside, if you kept to yourself, didn't look at anyone for more than a glance, and didn't want to make a name for yourself, you got left alone. But the heightened awareness of time, the sudden realisations at three am of where he actually was, and the profound lack of privacy made him want the freedom to be anonymous, to be away from people when he needed to be, and the choice of being with those he wanted to be with.

He had a beer in a pub he once drank at in the city, not because he was tonguing for it, or for any reminiscence, but because the beer symbolised freedom, and the alcohol let him believe it. He rang Ronnie from the blue pay-phone next to the cigarette machine. Ronnie was hungover but willing, in his need for a day-after session, to meet him at another bar, at the other end of the train line, closer to his home.

The west opened up for him. Bands of industry and unemployment spread out from the train window. And the beer, or the thought of more, and putting his feet up on the opposite seat, gave him hope for his first day out.

The walk from the station to the pub where he was to meet Ronnie worked off any lingering beer. Inside the ashen pub there was a group he recognised sitting at a table. They were people he went to high school with. He looked away. He would wait for Ronnie outside.

—Whitey!

Ronnie was at that table. Because they were Whitey's friends. And Ronnie's. He hadn't realised — or at least, didn't want to. Because now he'd have to explain shit he wasn't ready to talk about. He hadn't processed his time inside for long enough to express it with the posturing his mates might expect.

But time had made them not care. And alcohol, wetting the ash at the table, had diluted their interest in others. So he drank the few that he was shouted, and hugged Ronnie in the toilets after a piss, and skulled shots of tequila at the bar with him. And they all left for Ronnie's with cases under their arms, or half-gone cans, or a bottle of scotch. Because they wanted music and yelling — takeaway things.

Shock was beginning to set in. Because of the beer, the behaviour, and the big line of goey that he'd roughly dragged up into his sinuses.

Back at Ronnie's house, his wife was waiting with a child, a girl, and a baby they'd had while Whitey was away. A boy. Helen, the eldest, couldn't speak when Whitey'd gone in, and it seemed that she was still unable to. She knew language though, and was happy with just knowing.

—She remembers ya, Whitey. Don't ya, Helen? Michelle said.

—She's quiet, he remarked.

—Oh, she's all right. Aren't ya, baby?

Inside the fibro house, Whitey pushed her around on the plastic dump truck, dodging the sparse furniture and thick people. Then he was sitting on the back step, drinking harsh unaged scotch, and drawing hard on a Winnie Red — there was no smoking inside the house.

—So. How've you been? she asked as she shifted in next to him.

Whitey looked at her, and drew again. Natalie. Nat. Like everyone here she looked like a new version — or an older version — of the person he remembered. As he was to her, he supposed.

—Okay, he said, and smiled, and fumbled for the chipped glass.

—Happy? Ya know, ta be out?

—Yeah.

—So, what was it like?

—Okay. I mean ya learn ta handle. Ya havta.

—Listen. I um found out that that Eddie guy, the guy I brought 'round, he was a pig. I swear, Whitey, I didn't know. I swear. Looking back, I mean, his fucking haircut, but please believe me.

—I believe you. I knew he was a pig but didn't twig until too late too. Way too fucking late!

—Can you forgive me?

—Hmm? I dunno, Caxaro.

Nat looked down at her shoes.

—Hey, I'm kiddin'. Fuckit. I said I believe you. Forget it. Of course I forgive you.

Whitey had thought about it a lot inside. The Eddie fucker had fooled him. And it just didn't seem like the type of thing Nat would do to him. He just couldn't see her going to those lengths to fuck him up. Whitey slid his hand up Nat's back, and rubbed her shoulders.

—Hey, Whitey, you know I thought about you, and — she put her head between her knees — and I touched myself, a few times.

—I did too, about you, but more than a few times, he said, and drank off the scotch; he was smooth now.

He hugged her. And they kissed, twisting their backs on the step. They went inside. In Helen's room, amongst the curled and knotted-blonde nylon and flesh-coloured vinyl dolls, they lay on the single bed Helen didn't use — she and her baby brother both slept with their parents. Whitey and Nat bit and licked each other's teeth and pulled at each other's shirts. Nat was chubby, had gotten chubbier maybe, he thought. She was Maltese and her skin was all one perfect colour, except on the small of her back, where Whitey'd come every time they'd had sex. She'd cut and streaked her hair while he was away — probably several times. Her eyes were so brown they were almost black and he could easily see the whites in the darkness. He could like her. She was a chocolate girl.

He scratched at her bra and she unhooked it. He rolled off her panties. Her vagina gave off a heat he'd almost forgotten and he dripped to be inside it. She was unshaven and looked like Vegemite toast, cut diagonally. He sucked in her labia and swallowed, but she pulled his head up.

—Fuck me, she said to his cheek. He entered her and could feel the spasm arcing through his groin. He withdrew and she grabbed him and bent him back inside. He thrust hard, slamming her along the Wiggles sheets, the violence stifling his come. The speed he'd taken pushed and aggressed until the semen burst into her, his orgasm coming only when he was empty and kissing her.

They lay and leaked.

—You've never done that before. Come inside me, she said, her mouth struggling with saliva.

—Sorry.

—I prefer it. It's more like making love, you know, she said, a bit too close to his ear.

He turned his head to face her.

—So did you, um, get any sex inside?

—I told you, I just jerked off thinking of you a hell of a lot, he said, and touched her stomach.

She flinched, for ticklishness and a loathing of having that part of her touched.

But he had had sex in prison. Or, at least, he had shared his male need. Pulling at an uncircumcised cock, wanting the thick spit of semen as much as its owner. And had had his own blunt cock brought to an orgasm like that of early pubescence. It was a turn-on. There was no need for physical attraction; it was all about coming. Until the cold after-burn.

—So what about you? he asked. Got a boyfriend?

—Kinda.

—What does that mean?

—I see a guy. Sometimes, she said, and looked away.

—Oh.

He got some beers for them, but Nat had fallen asleep. He sat there drinking, tired, but the goey wouldn't let him sleep; until he did.

The speed was still at work in him when he woke a few hours later. Purple light was leaking into the fibro. Natalie's skin was less perfect now, but he was hard. His kisses made her roll away. She was lying face down now, and he climbed on top of her. He tried to insert himself but she closed her legs. He left the room and jerked himself to a quick orgasm in the toilet.

The evidence was too much throughout the house. People and carpet, both lying lumpy, smelt of beer. Helen was awake and testing cans for dregs.

He took her out into the backyard where they climbed the old ghost gum and watched the sun threaten over the steel and tile. And magpies talked of the coming day.

The flat was on the ground floor and had a small courtyard. Easy to break into. Not that his things were worth a forced pane or broken glass. His possessions had been kept by the Public Trustees Office while he was away — released to him by paying a tax — and no longer felt they were his. They had the smell of the not-too-distant past though, which came back in intensely short gusts. He set his things up — spacing them evenly through the one room. The mattress, the foam two-seater, the three drawers, the low table, the portable telly and its cousin, the portable stereo.

He'd also gone back into business. He'd been offered five ounces of head on credit, and a few days later, two ounces of gooey. For a drug dealer, living in Brunei was like having a souvenir shop at the airport outside the JAL terminal.

Ronnie had also lent him the use of an unregistered VB Commodore to run around in. The rectangle of yellow new-growth grass where the car had been almost permanently stalled was too poignant for Whitey as they rolled the freshly-jumped

Holden onto the street. Would going back to his life before prison burn him, the way it had before, the way the sun had laid waste to the grass outside the shade of the Commodore? He didn't want to think about it. But things were rolling.

FIVE

Sonja lay on the grass, letting it etch into the back of her thighs. She put her arm over her eyes, making the inside of her elbow fit snugly over the bridge of her nose, to shield them from the lunchtime sun. She disappeared from the sun, from the other students, from time.

She heard the grass telling her of an approach. She lifted her sun-sealed arm but her eyelids knew better and strained in a shaky protest.

—Hey, someone said.

Sonja sat up, into the wood of someone's skull and dropped back onto the now hard and indifferent grass.

Sonja vomited into the plastic bucket. A boy was already on the sickbay bed, so Sonja sat hunched in the vinyl chair. The boy whose head had knocked her down looked into the doorway.

—It was a mistake, he said. I thought you were someone else. My head got hurt too.

The deputy principal called him into the office.

—We've called your mother, the office lady said. She'll be 'ere when she can get 'ere, she told us.

Sonja worried how her mother would get to the school. They didn't have a car. And she was sure she wouldn't know the way anyway. It had been her father who'd enrolled them. But the worry was thick and numb, unlike the usual sharpness that accompanied anxiety concerning her family. She'd forgotten twice now why she was in the sickbay. And she felt sleepy. But then that hotness would spurt up, making her vomit and vomit. She dreamed for a while, about the sickbay and the school office, and the orchard beyond. How it went neglected, while the dramas echoed through the halls and offices.

—Sonja. Your mother's come for you, the office lady said, shaking her too hard.

And her mother was before her. With a man. A young man. An absolutely beautiful young man. He was nervous, and dressed in that shabby, heavily faded, Aussie way, but not the deliberate way the boys here tried for. His clothes were his. He was boyish and slouching, but she could see something manly in his out-of-place stance — he wasn't trying to cover up his nervousness by acting tough like a teenager. What was he doing here with her mother?

—Sonja, what has happened? her mother asked, thankfully in English.

—I think I was hit on the head.

—We'll take you to the hospital now.

—Who's we, mother?

—Ah, this is, ah — the young man who lives in the next stairs over. I heard his car when the school called and asked him to drive me. He has taken me, bless him, and will to the hospital now.

The young man looked at her and smiled. He looked tired and confused. It was how she felt too.

★

In the casualty ward Whitey was tapping his foot with indecision. People would be knocking on his door, wanting to score, and then kicking it, and going around the back to look in — to wake him, or get in and turn the place over. Maybe. There were plenty of other dealers at Brunei. He didn't want to leave, or to say he had to leave. So he stood. And shook his leg. And bit his cheek. Katerina Marmeladova thanked him and did something with her mouth, like she was about to talk, and then did it again. He liked this lady. The trip to the school had been a bit uncomfortable, but he liked the fact that she was a mother, living of all places at Brunei Court, and he was able to help. And her daughter, the reason he was here: he was fascinated. Both by her, and by his reaction to her. She was a school chick, and sick, but she was striking. When they had walked into the sickbay, he'd seen some boy on the bed, and that uncomfortable feeling from the ride over had escalated, but when the mother started talking to the girl sitting in the chair, the feeling swung. It wasn't comfortable, but it was something he wanted more of.

—Concussion, Dr Keshvardoust said. Don't let her sleep this afternoon. Plenty of fluids. I've given her an injection for the vomiting.

The doctor smiled evenly at Whitey, because who else could he be but a big brother? He smiled back. But his smile, unlike the one it mimicked, lacked medicine degrees, supportive parents, and proud aunties and uncles back in Syria. He wandered off, to let any further conversation carry on unhindered by his misplacement.

★

—Thank you, Sonja said in the front seat of the Commodore, because neither of the back windows wound down. By the way, my name is Sonja.

—I know, he said. Your mother told me.

She was still pale, but a peachiness had returned to her cheeks, and Whitey found it hard to keep his eyes off her. She looked up at him, her head angled down slightly. Her eyes were too bright to look into and drive. The dull road was much less intrusive.

At Brunei, he put his hand on her back to help her up the stairs, and left for his own flat to the sound of their gratitude, saying:

—No worries, hope ya feel better.

He was flushed with new feelings he liked — they gave him an energy — but that he wished to purge, because he couldn't identify them.

The days of supposedly increased choices fell into one another. He did sit-ups and push-ups, for lack of the prison gym. He watched what was on the telly. People came over to score. Some sat, had a smoke, got paranoid, and left. Others left straightaway, and he could hear them talking to whomever had chucked in with them in the stairwell, examining and debating size and aroma. He only sold to those he knew well now, but he was also aware that customers inevitably made introductions. It was hard to tell with speed buyers. But, he reasoned, pot buyers could be trusted. And six months had taught him not to explore offers of purchases of ozs of goey — or H.

Natalie came over. They fucked, rolling around on the foam between knocks at the door. And though he'd never had feelings for her before, now he started to dislike her. For her condescension. For her well-meaning — he supposed — instructions on how life is in the post-jail age; how life should, could, be for him. And the way she began each sentence with So.

—So, why did you start dealing again? she asked.
—I dunno. Because I was asked, I guess.
—Shouldn't you worry about getting busted. Again?
—Yeah.

But he didn't worry. Or at least he'd reasoned with the worry. People had always put too much faith in him — in his judgment and his self-confidence. Saw in him something he couldn't see in himself. He'd been able, on a number of occasions, to threaten — effectively — when there was just no violence in him to back it up. It was the same with selling. People thought he should do it, so he did — on the strength of others' opinions. He was, it seemed, shackled with an image, a persona, with a will of its own, that knew how to act, whereas he'd actually never learned. But it did at least tow him along in life.

And it wasn't Nat's hypocritical questioning of his dealing or his life outside that really bothered him — she smoked his cones and dipped into the goey — it was her presumption that he wanted her advice and opinions. Or even her vagina, or her presence.

She said he was sulky since he'd gotten out.

But he didn't dislike her enough to ask her not to come around anymore — he couldn't have given her a real reason anyway — so he stayed sulky, and ignorant, and withdrew.

SIX

His car was in the carport, as it had been on the several other occasions Sonja had walked towards his flat, but had found small reasons in the asphalt not to go further. It was the only car to be seen within at least six carports — that is, of course, except for the police cruisers that came and went with alarming regularity. She hadn't seen him since the hospital. Maybe he'd moved and left his car. She hoped not. She wanted to know someone, someone who lived here; and he'd been so close. And she hadn't been able to stop thinking about him at all. And the fact that he lived so close — actually in this same block of unattractive flats — was driving her wild. She'd felt so confused, and then depressed, after that day with Raz. It'd been, as she predicted, the last time they spoke, let alone spent time together. For a while she thought she might love Raz, because she couldn't stop thinking about him. But eventually, and a bit disappointingly, she realised it was simply that — although she'd never ask him — she wanted to know what he thought of her, why he'd acted so bizarrely. But since the day of the hospital, any thought of Raz was totally eclipsed. This new boy had cured her of him. And filled her with a new set of feelings that burned hotter, but were much more positive than those Raz had caused her to suffer.

So she climbed the steps — uncomfortably identical to the ones leading to her own door — and knocked, wincing with what could be such a naive act. She could see no movement through the peephole, but could sense it. The door opened.

—Hi, he said, and then, as though the gods were watching, she thought, Sonja, is it?

He didn't seem as tall, but darker, and with much bluer eyes than she'd remembered from that day in his car.

—Yeah, hi. I don't actually know your name, she said, and was unexpectedly pleased with her response which seemed so mature and clear.

—Oh, it's Patrick. Sorry, I thought I told your mum.

—You probably did. She forgets Australian names.

—Well, I hope there hasn't been another accident. He smiled with one side of his mouth.

—No, no. I, um, just wanted to thank you, you know, properly, and to get you something, but I didn't know what to get.

—No, nothing. You don't need to get me anything. We're neighbours, right? he said, maybe reddening a little, Sonja saw.

—Please. My mum insists, Sonja lied. We thought maybe a case of beer.

—A case? No. Maybe a bottle, he said, leaning further out the doorway.

—What about a bottle of wine then?

—No, no, it's all right.

—Please? she laughed, bending her knees in mock frustration.

—Okay, but ya really don't have to.

—Red or white?

—Um, red. The cheapest. Honestly.

He rubbed his stomach, maybe nervously, under his T-shirt, and she saw the trickle of hair running from his navel into his jeans.

—Okay, well, I'll see you soon, Patrick, she said, and backed away.

—Okay, bye, Sonja. Nice to see ya well, too.

—Thanks.

She hit the bottom of the steps and suddenly thought that maybe she'd left too quickly, like a schoolgirl. Maybe she should have stayed a while more, extended the conversation. But then, Patrick did seem to be a man of few words.

People he didn't know always seemed to drive him to politeness. Now he would have to accept a gift from this girl, which would have to lead to more politeness, which made him a little uncomfortable. But as he sat back down on his two-seater, and sifted some heads and tobacco between his thumb and index finger, he realised that the polite exchange he'd just had was more satisfying — he could still feel a lingering burn of endorphin — than the unchanging lump of words he and his mates (customers) dropped at each other's feet.

Someone knocked on his door. Westie, after two sticks and a half-weight.

SEVEN

It was a risk, driving around in an unregistered 1979 particoloured — thanks to several transplanted panels — Commodore with bulk drugs. He only felt this on his third pick-up though, because he was only just beginning to get over the authority that went with driving again. It was probably more of a risk walking with the drugs anyway. He picked them up from Ronnie's place. And Ronnie got a quarter oz — which he sold — for letting Whitey use his place for the exchange.

Waldo, who always brought along his dog, was — at least as far as Whitey knew — the source of the drugs. The heeler-cross sat and examined his fleas and the damage they'd done to his sheath. He relaxed everyone. Helen mimicked the counting and weighing, right down to the dipping and licking. And the ignition and blowing-out-the-window of the bong smoke.

Waldo and the heeler were happy. One drunk and speeding, the other thoroughly content. Ronnie stood with his beer, maybe ready to run — if there was a cop-knock. Whitey drank, because the freshly opened case on the floor looked so inviting, with its photograph of a crisp-looking, perpetually full beer bottle. They laughed about school. But Whitey didn't really remember Waldo from those days, except that they'd both shared unfortunate acne and an English class. There were no laughs between them then. But now, there was micro-capitalism. Laughs of the small-businessmen.

Waldo left after a phone call from his missus filled him with doubt and his speed hit visibly skipped a beat. Whitey and Ronnie drank the rest of the case with speedy, flared nostrils. And were amazed at each other's power of chemically sharpened mimicry of mutual acquaintances.

Afterwards, he dropped Ronnie at the bottleshop, but Whitey had to get back to Brunei because of the promises weighed and bagged under the back seat of the car.

The act of getting drugs from the car to the flat had to be covert, but the best he could manage was an outdated sports bag. The bag was quickly dropped and unburdened, the stash of drugs replenished in their various locations in the toilet/laundry. Not so much hidden from a bust, but from customers. Pot in the toilet-brush holder; gooey under the twin tub.

He dropped another fingerful of speed, then tidied up. Clothes, dishes — which made him realise that he hadn't been eating for the last couple of days. And he wouldn't eat today. Hot doubt rushed with the speed of speed through his chest — a side effect of the drug he could never get used to. But someone knocked, a bit lightly, on his door.

Looking through the peephole, wondered who told this girl from up the next stairs, Sonja, that he sold. The speed allowed for quick, if not accurate thought. Maybe she isn't here to score — like last time.

—Hi, Patrick, she said. It sounded a bit like a question, so he answered:

—Yeah, Sonja.

—I just thought I'd bring this over. She held out the thickness of a bottle in brown paper.

—Cool, thank you. He motioned for her to come up the step she'd backed down.

She handed him the bottle her mother had bought.

—Do you wanna come in? he asked, because the stairwells at Brunei reverberated, and sound became like the graffiti — random and coarse.

—Okay.

He took the bottle out of the paper bag and looked at it, as if he knew something about wine. He was not sure how long he should keep looking at it.

—Thank you, he said. And thank your mum, too.

—I will, she said and leaned on the bench in his kitchenette.

—So how've you been? Head okay?

—Yeah, thanks. I started feeling better the next day.

—Good, good. So, how long have you lived here?

Sonja appeared nervous, and it was making him a little edgy too. But when she spoke his unease evaporated. Her voice was like nothing he'd heard — it was young, but not really a girl's voice, and that accent, whatever it was, it was so cute. He wanted to hear it more.

—Too long, she said. About two years. My dad's in hospital. But we're able to keep the flat.

—Oh. I'm sorry.

—That's okay.

—You like it here? Whitey asked.

—Nah. I don't know, it's a bit —

—Yeah, I know.

—Actually, I've got another favour to ask you, she said, looking down at the bench.

—Yeah, okay, but I've, um, got friends coming over, maybe.

—Oh.

—But ask me, he said, and leaned on the bench next to her.

—Okay. I've, um, got this assignment from school, for English. We have to write about our community. I was hoping I could ask you some questions about, you know, living here, in these flats.

—Sure, I guess, but I'm not sure I'm what you're after.

—But you're easy to talk to, I mean, think I can talk to you. Is it okay?

—Yeah, why not? Be fun to do some homework!

He opened the bottle while she went back home to get her assignment book. He drank half a tumblerful of the metallic wine and spat out some cork. The drink was quenching but hot. He found the soaked cork piece and put it in the sink. He would have to think of something to say to Sonja if anyone came to score. Or maybe he should just tell her the truth? He wanted to be honest with her. But he also wanted her to like him. Because he liked her. She kept getting prettier every moment he glanced at her. He had never been able to tell when girls liked him. It always seemed to come out of the blue. And when girls he had been into weren't attracted to him, it didn't really bother him. Of course it stabbed at first, but he was able to lose interest fairly quickly. But he wanted Sonja to like him. Did she? Or was she just a friendly girl, thanking him for the lift to the hospital? That seemed more likely. But he hoped that it was more. He hoped that she would come back with her assignment, like she said.

★

They sat at his coffee table, she on his two-seater, he on a cushioned milk crate. Maleness had shocked her nostrils when she'd come right into his flat. But it wasn't offensive. It was so his. And she hoped she wouldn't get used to it — it made her feel alive. She'd had to quickly draw up the English task, because it was a lie that had come to her in the moment. It was reasonable though. Her English teacher, and the careers counsellor, had told her to write about anything that she felt she should write about. Of course, they were encouraging her to attempt several scholarships when they'd suggested it, but this would be something she really wanted to write about. Since the hospital, Patrick had become such an inspiration. He was handsome, but not egotistical — as far as she could tell — he was independent, but looked quite young. He seemed a bit shy, and she found this so appealing when she thought about how the boys at school acted. And he lived here, in Brunei Court, where she thought only people with financial and social problems lived — Loserville, the kids at school called it. But Patrick wasn't a loser. He was an angel.

While she got ready to ask her first invented question, Sonja and Patrick smirked at each other. He poured another glass of wine.

—Would you like one? Oh. Sorry, are you old enough?

—No, um, not really, but I would like one.

He got her a glass.

—Will this be all right with ya mum?

—Yeah, she said, because it was too late now, and maybe her mother wouldn't care anyway. Maybe.

The bottle, a deep vein, was between them. Like cherries, or blood, the wine was on her lips and her teeth.

—So, she began, reading from a hastily manufactured script: where were you living and what were you doing before you moved here?

—Okay — And he told her.

His story was proved almost immediately when two guys came knocking. Bought some marijuana. Sonja witnessed a criminal act. But it seemed far removed from what she'd expected of a transaction deserving of jail time.

She asked to look at the drugs. She had never seen them before. They looked appealing, like food. She asked for another glass of wine.

—Now, you see. I don't think you can use me as your, um, interviewee.

—Well, no. I guess I can't tell my teacher. I don't want to get you in trouble.

—Sorry. I know it's probably heavy for you. I don't know why I agreed to talk to you. But I did want you to come back. So —

—Thank you, Patrick. And it's not really heavy. I mean, it kind of is, but now that I've seen it, you know, drug dealing, it's not heavy at all.

—Ya know, I don't usually like people calling me Patrick, everyone calls me Whitey, but I like the way it sounds when you say it.

He poured them each a glass of wine.

—Patrick, she said.

—Jesus, now we're getting too deep, he said, and they both laughed.

He took another sip of the still-coursing wine. He leaned back on the crate, supporting himself with his arms behind him, his hands, veined with dark wineblood, spread on the floor. She saw the trickle of hair below his navel again. His eyes were closed, but his mouth was open. She was a little drunk. She'd never felt drunk before. She'd had wine, even vodka, but it had just made her sleepy. This was the opposite. This was an awakening. Patrick looked so beautiful. He smelt so delicious. She knew she could fall in love with him. She knew she already had. Whereas an hour ago it was an intense but unidentifiable feeling, now it was omnipresent, and nothing could be more right. She leaned across the two-seater and had to drop a bare knee to the floor. She kissed him on the mouth, quickly, and then again, long enough to taste his wine. He brought himself forward and looked at her, maybe a bit shocked, but he smiled and kissed her back. He moved so his arm was around her waist and she between his legs. He kissed her again and the wine, separated into tumblers a few minutes before, was re-flowing in their mouths.

His breath was hot, and his body so hard and strong. His face was soft as he moved from kissing her mouth to all over her face. And her neck. It drove her crazy. She was no longer drunk.

Her little black-and-red dress had bunched up on her thighs, and she could see him looking at her panties. Tutti-frutti they said. She wondered why she'd worn them. They were so little-girly. She took them off — she felt like they would burn if they didn't come off — and pulled the dress over her head between his kisses.

—Take your shirt off, she demanded. She couldn't believe she'd said it. A new her had taken over. One that she hadn't even met an hour ago.

She saw that the trickle of hair on his stomach was alone on his skin. Until he rolled off his jeans.

—Are you sure? he said.

—Do I feel it? she said.

She rubbed her readiness on the top of his thigh. And he was inside her, and kissing her. It hurt. He pushed it so hard and fast. But the pain was soothed as he kept pushing. Slower, but with a passion she would never have imagined a man could have.

—What about — should I stop? he asked.

—Please, no, she said.

He lifted her body up to him. And breathed hard in her ear. He said her name. And eased her back onto the floor. He stayed on top of her. Moving much slower now. It felt incredible, and she wished it would last forever. But after a few more minutes he took it out. It hurt more when he took it out. But he hugged her until his breathing slowed again.

—*Jesus*, he said, running his hand through his hair while leaning on his elbow. I'm sorry.

—Why? Can we hug again, please?

He lay back down next to her, and she could feel his arm.

—I'm too, um, old for you, he said. Sorry, I like you. Really like you. But you don't want to know how old I am, and I don't want to know how young you are.

—I'm sixteen, she said.

—I'm twenty-six, he said.

They were able to hug some more then, and even kiss. And finish the wine, and have sex again.

EIGHT

Whitey lay on the floor where he'd woken, where he must have passed out the night before. His mind tracked backward, trying to sort through flashes of what had happened the previous day. He'd gone to the bottleshop, and had been drinking cask wine alone. Either celebrating or drowning something. No. He'd been drinking to absorb shock. He'd never had an afternoon like that. That girl, Sonja. Fuck. Sonja. He looked at where they'd had sex. It made him feel horny — not in the usual hangover-bustin'-for-a-quick-hot-orgasm-just-for-a-moment-of-pleasure/escape horniness — but a smooth, genuine endorphin-filled horniness. He looked at the ceiling and smiled.

She's only sixteen.

And all that speed, all that alcohol turned in him.

He sat up and tested the cask. He filled the glass. And smelt Sonja.

He lay back down and pulled the doona off his mattress. It had her on it and he breathed it, and breathed it. Tears stung his eyes with their toxicity, but he had to masturbate, and for the first time in his memory he thought of only one woman.

Or girl.

NINE

The intravenous drip was full, which meant that the nurse had only just been. So if her father appeared to be asleep, Sonja knew he was feigning. She wanted her father to be awake; she wanted to talk to him.

—Dad, she said, and touched his arm. Hi, Dad, how are you feeling today?

Zakhar rolled towards his daughter and gave her a small snarl. Sonja knew the snarl was not aimed at her. It was his self-disappointment. He'd told her, when they'd been alone during her last visit, that it finally didn't matter if he drank anymore or not. But he no longer felt like it. The surgeons had removed that part of his liver that made him thirst, he'd said. And the years he'd spent in Australia had been thoroughly wasted.

Sonja kissed her father's forehead.

—Mum just took Peter to the toilet, she said.

He nodded and pulled himself higher up the bed.

—Dad, she continued. I don't even know how to say this. I want to have a boyfriend. Sonja had thought about it all night and all morning between snatches of sleep in which she could feel herself smiling. She had to tell someone about Patrick. But she didn't want to tell her mother, not just yet. In case her mother couldn't handle it. But her father, although he'd been compulsive with alcohol, was much more in control of his emotions. She could at least trust him — particularly as he was in a hospital bed — to react without succumbing to fits of yelling and tears.

Zakhar regarded her now. His eyes had the look of a child; a child much younger than his daughter. He looked away.

—I don't think your mother will allow.

—I haven't asked her. I wanted to know how you feel, Sonja said, but couldn't look at him now either.

—Boys, Sonja, he sighed. Boys can be friends, but boys can be friendly because they want something that is not friendship.

—What about older boys? Or men? she asked.

—I don't know, Sonja. I think there is little change from boys to men.

—But some men must love their girlfriends.

—A man is something you will have to wait for, Sonja.

Sonja's mother, brother and sister walked into the ward.

—I like someone, Dad, and I think he likes me, she whispered, and glanced at her mother, hoping she hadn't heard.

Sonja liked the smell of the hospital. And the hospital staff looked happy today. She walked through the corridors. She wanted to get lost in them. Yesterday she'd made love. She'd really made love. It'd felt stranger and nicer than she'd imagined. It was so — so physical. The part when he put it in. She could still feel him there. And his body on hers. His muscles tensed over every part of her. And lying, smiling at each other.

But did he love her?

It wasn't like with Raz; but it could end up like the Raz thing had — nodding at her the first time he'd seen her after their — what? Fling? Affair? Whatever it was — and then never even looking at her again for the rest of the term.

Would she see Patrick again? How would it be? How could another situation be created where they could spend that sort of time together? Would her parents allow her to see him again if they found out what she'd done with Patrick? She wanted them to know. But Patrick was a man. A man. She had a man. Or, at least, she'd had a man. She couldn't bear not seeing him again.

TEN

Natalie looked at the small bag of heads she'd just bought. She'd hoped to smoke some of it with Whitey, but he'd simply handed it to her at the door and told her he was way too hungover to smoke. His flat smelt of sex. He could have at least told her. *Just* like when they were seeing each other before he went to jail: he'd just stopped. Stopped calling her, stopped talking to her when they ran into one another, and given no explanation. Well, it seemed now she'd gotten an explanation. He was fucking someone else. She put the bag in her pocket as three guys got on the train and sat across from her.

—Hey, one of the guys said.

—Hey.

—Goin' in ta town? he asked, nodding in a north-easterly direction.

—Nah, she said. Just heading home. She shifted a little.

—Where's home?

—Wentworthville.

—With ya boyfriend?

—Pft. Boyfriend. Nah, I live with my mum.

—What nationality are ya?

—What do ya mean? Aussie, she said.

—Ya look Italian or somethin'.

—My parents are Maltese, Natalie said, and pulled her shirt down over her slightly exposed stomach. She could feel their eyes on it. It made her feel cold.

—Maltese. But ya call yourself Aussie, hey? We're Lebs. Ah, except this bloke, he's a choco, but he's a Leb in trainin', he said and ruffled the younger guy's hair.

—Oh, she said. The 'choco' was cute.

—So, do ya smoke pot? the speaker asked.

—I dunno. Do you? she shrugged.

—Fuckin' A, the cute one said, the subject seeming to give him the confidence to talk. His attempt at a moustache was still soft, feminine, like the hair on her arms — but he was definitely on the way to being good-looking.

—Have you got any? she asked.

—Always, baby, the original talker answered.

—Hmm, Nat said, and smiled at the cute one. She'd been hanging out for a smoke, but she didn't like smoking on her own much. Her mind would tear off in sometimes worrying directions when there was no company to make her laugh. And if these guys supplied the pot, she could save her stash for later.

—We should go for a smoke. What's ya name, baby? the guy asked.

—Buffy, Nat said, because all this attention made her feel like the vampire slayer.

They got off at Lidcombe Station and walked a few blocks to a car detailer's workshop. The more confident guy's car was there having new seats installed.

—What was wrong with the old seats? Nat asked.

—They're not as cool as these new ones, he told her. And I still got extra money from my car loan ta blow.

They got in the car and headed for a place where the guys said they could have a quiet, undisturbed smoke. They seemed to be heading back west, but a way Nat wasn't familiar with. She looked around at the guys from her position in the back seat, trying to read their expressions. It felt weird, being so close to these guys, in this little car, when she didn't know them at all. She couldn't read them. And they weren't talking. They wound through back streets and Nat got glimpses of things she thought she recognised: a corner store, a novelty letterbox. Until they parked. They were in the carpark of a public pool. But it was clearly no longer used. The garden surrounding the building was oversized and growing into shapes that no council gardener would have allowed. The boys said they smoked here all the time; that it'd be cool, that no one came down here. Nat wasn't quite sure which pool it was. She wasn't much of a pool kid growing up.

They passed the carapace of the building that was once the ice-skating rink, and their voices echoed through the smashed windows. Two of the boys talked in Arabic, humourlessly. The cute one, who didn't seem to understand the language either, looked at Nat. Then one of the other guys took out his mobile phone and began talking in Arabic, now with a bit more animation. It relaxed Nat a bit, as she'd begun to think that the guys' moods had altered since they'd got here — they seemed to be in a hurry to get to the place where they'd have the session. But she didn't feel like smoking with them anymore.

At the initial-carved barbecue benches that families once used when eating their hot chips with water-wrinkled fingers, a joint was passed around. Nat refused a toke on the first round, but on the second was forced to explain.

—Have some, one of the guys urged.

—Nah, I don't really feel like it now, she said.

—Huh? Have some. You said ya wanted some. Have a toke.

—No, really, I might just head home actually, Natalie said, and stood up.

—Huh? Sit down, babe. C'mon, relax. We won't bite.

—Hmm. I'll stay for a little while, but I don't want any pot, really. She sat back down. She noticed something switch on in the guy's eyes when she made to leave, something she wanted to avoid seeing again. Going along with him seemed to stop it.

—Sure, the more confident one said. Sure, it's up to you. It's good stuff. You're pretty hot, ya know.

—Thanks. But now I know you've had too much pot, Nat giggled, trying some artificial sweetener on the situation. Anything to stop him from looking at her again with that expression in his eyes.

—Nuh. So, have ya ever gone out with a Leb? he asked.

—No, I don't really know any.

—So, would ya like to have a Lebanese boyfriend? Ya know we're the best lovers in the world. Ya'll never go back after ya've had Leb-style, he said, and they all laughed.

—I don't really judge a guy by his nationality.

—Well ya know Leb guys are fuckin' well-hung, do ya judge on that?

Natalie didn't answer. She looked at the cute one. She tried to half smile at him, but she was feeling too out of herself to manage it. This place, these boys. She wanted to leave. If she could just avoid his eyes. Just get up and leave. These guys would follow her though; and they were right, no one came here — not one person had come by.

—I might head off now, guys.

—C'mon, babe, the confident one said, and grabbed her around the waist. He pushed her hair back behind her ears and kissed her cheek, then licked it. Then his hand was down the back of her jeans, grabbing her g-string.

Then the other one, the other Lebanese one, was cupping her breast with tensed fingers. The confident one undid the button of her jeans and Natalie pushed his hand away.

—'Ey, fuckin' bitch, he snarled.

—Fu — Fuck, Natalie gasped, and she was crying. She hadn't felt it coming, the crying was sudden.

—Charlie, get the fuck over here, the confident one said to the young one. Hold her.

She felt the guy's arms wrap around her. The other two pulled her jeans off. There were hands all over her vagina, fingers cutting into her. They were pulling at her undies, but somehow she managed to keep them from coming all the way off. Someone was yelling in the distance. Natalie shut her eyes.

—Abdullah, ya dirty bastard, she heard more clearly now, and the hands were off her. She opened her eyes. She could smell them, these guys. They smelt of an almost-feminine cologne, stale sweat and marijuana. The one who'd pushed her down, whose hot breath she'd felt in her throat, was motioning or waving or something. There were more guys coming. The other Lebanese guy stood on the barbecue table and yelled something in Arabic. The other one whistled. Natalie stood and ran. They'd pulled off her shoes with her jeans. She hadn't even felt it. She ran. She ran away from the guys, away from the barbecue table, her jeans, her shoes, her wallet.

The guys were yelling. She ran towards the other end of the now-filled-in pool, and through a gap in the cyclone-wire fence. There must be some shops, some houses.

The lighting was way too harsh in the little interview room. They'd given her a blanket, and Natalie sat there with it wrapped around her in her T-shirt, socks and undies until her mother arrived with some pants. A female cop had sat with her, but Natalie was barely aware of her. When her mother turned up, another cop, a man, wanted to talk to her. He said, to start with, just to tell him in her own words, in her own time, what had happened. It was hard to know what to tell them. Her mother kept crying and looking away from her; she seemed pissed off about the guys getting hold of the wallet, knowing her address now.

—One's name was Abdullah, she began.
—Abdullah, the female cop repeated.
—Yes.
—And the younger one, I think they called him Chris, or — Charlie. They said he wasn't Lebanese. Italian I think. They called him a choco.

She couldn't remember what they looked like. Like any other bunch of guys. Not westies though. They wore those clothes that are meant to look cool but don't. One was wearing a European or Pommie soccer shirt. She could remember the more confident guy's expressions. And his smell. My god, please don't let me smell that cologne again, she pleaded. She seemed to reek of it herself though. She wanted to vomit. They'd gotten her a bucket. But the vomit wouldn't come. Like the rest of her, her stomach was paralysed. And then she realised there was a name for why she was here, why they were about to take her to the hospital, why the lady in the four-wheel-drive she'd flagged down had so readily let her into her new Landcruiser and brought her here: rape. She'd escaped. But nevertheless, she was a victim of rape. It was something she'd worried about, like any woman, but she'd never imagined she'd be an actual victim of it. Never.

ELEVEN

Senior Sergeant Testafiglia motioned for his sergeant to enter the office. Sergeant Rosales hadn't been Testafiglia's first choice. He was Filipino, and as he was the only Asian officer he'd ever worked with, Testafiglia had been dubious about his policing skills. Statistically, there were very few Asians on the force, and Testafiglia had thought that there must be a reason for this. But it seemed the Cebuano police are trained tough and honest, and Rosales had become Testafiglia's favourite officer on the day-shift. He was a family man, had four daughters, and knew the value of keeping family together by having rules and boundaries.

Rosales moved in and took the seat across from his boss.

—One name with priors did come up, he began.

—Do we know him? Testafiglia asked.

—Patrick White. We busted him for possession with intent to sell. He got eighteen months and was let out after six for good behaviour. Miss Caxaro, as you remember, was part of the set-up for his bust. The detective never revealed to her that he was a cop, but it's more than possible this White believes she set him up. She says she visited him about an hour before the attack. She had a sexual relationship with him. I think we should watch him. This could be revenge, boss. May not be linked to the other rapes. Or he could be the drug link. Supplying the drugs and even tipping off the attackers about girls who smoke marijuana.

—I remember White. Unsatisfying arrest, Testafiglia said.

—Yeah, didn't say yes, didn't say no. Could have more to hide. I suggest a surveillance. Simple day-watch to start with, no overtime.

—Keep me informed. I think you're on the right track here, Testafiglia said.

TWELVE

Sonja's body was the most pure, delicious, aromatic, narcotic, addictive thing. It existed just to fill him with the strongest, most insatiable appetite. But since she'd knocked on his door again, he hadn't eaten much more than human hair. Whitey found it hard to believe when he thought too hard about it, but his luck had changed. He was lucky to have met Sonja, and incredibly lucky that she liked him. He was totally beyond understanding her existence and his unbelievably close proximity to it. There was the age difference thing. But he only thought of this when they were apart, and Sonja had never brought it up. Whitey was on the verge of having something he'd never even hoped for. A relationship where he was in love with the other person.

She came to him daily, after school, and that was six periods too many. Sometimes they'd make love at lunchtime.

Whitey had drugs, and more cash to buy booze and groceries than he'd ever had before, but the smell of the top of Sonja's head was all he needed for sustenance. They lived off the richness of each other, and drank sweat. His foam mattress was heaven, and it floated above and beyond Colyton, Mt Druitt and north-east of there. He liked to eat her lips at the door at four-oh-two pm, and have her lower spine totally devoured by five.

—Fuck me. I love you, Sonja said.

—Oh, Jesus, you, he sighed.

All that romantic shit; it was true. All those books, all those movies; the authors had gotten a whiff of Sonja. Every single mole, every single hair was love. Sonja was an eclipse. He couldn't get enough of her, but he kept wondering: why did she keep on coming?

He had overwhelming bouts of doubt when she wasn't there. Was her love for him all some kind of warped practical joke to be televised after some clever editing? Or was it some other type of set-up?

Or was she just young?

THIRTEEN

Human Society and its Environment had been one of Sonja's favourite classes, but she couldn't recall one word that Ms Hunter had said to the class in the last three weeks. She'd sensed they were steering towards the Middle East and Islam lately, but it was peripheral to what really mattered.

Patrick. There really was nothing else. School just punctuated, for way, way too long, the real, beautiful, and totally fulfilling purpose of her life. Patrick. God, the way he touched her. There was soft electricity in his hands. And his smell. She could live in it. She'd taken one of his T-shirts and slept with it draped over her head. And hugged it in the morning. And when he kissed her everywhere, and was inside her, that was what life was about. It was all love. He was a man, but not like her father. She'd seen him drink, but he put down his drink without a second thought in order to hold and drink her.

She wanted to wake up next to him. She wanted to live with him.

But Polly and Peter. And her mother. Her mother didn't know yet. Mum could ruin the whole thing.

FOURTEEN

Abdullah Najib loved to drive. And he loved to drive when he was whacked. It was insane fun, tearing around the streets where the councils had yet to lay speed humps, stoned and zipping on speed. The speed. Last time he was on the zip he couldn't get a hard-on. He was planning to bring it up with the boys, see if it happened to any of them. But he hadn't worked out how to broach it yet.

He pumped the horn. Abdullah Najib didn't get out of the car, especially if he was driving. He saw the venetian blinds in the front window of Pinhead's house bend. Pinhead's mum looking out. Fuckin' bitch, he thought. Thinks that her son, fuckin' Pinhead, is too good to hang out with me. Fuckin' Abdullah Najib. Cunt's lucky I hang with him. Abdullah didn't call Pinhead Pinhead to his face; none of them did. Not because any of the boys were scared of him. Just because it was slack — the guy did have a long, thin head. But he was funny to be with. And always thinking about pussy. To his face the boys called him Fadi.

Fadi Mobahad slammed the front door and nodded slightly at Abdullah's metallic-blue Subaru WRX. He saw the tinted driver's side window roll down slightly, and knew he'd have to go and cop some shit at the window before he got in.

—Fuckin' mum lettin' ya out? Abdullah asked.

—Yeah, mate. What about your mum?

—What about my mum?

—Nuthin'.

—Let's go and pick up my bitch, Abdullah said.

The bong was passed between the WRX's Recaro seats. You had to be careful not to spill any bong water or let a burning pot seed come flying out of the cone. The WRX was cool, but it made you paranoid. Because it was Abdullah's, Ali Nora thought, and passed the bong back. The cone wasn't fully smoked, but he was too stoned already. He was the last of the crew to be picked up before the session, and this made him paranoid as well. It was like coming in on the end of a joke and no one will tell you what it's about. And today Abdullah had brought his new missus too, so both Ali and Fadi were in the back seat. Mia was hot, but a bit stuck up. Italian; I'd only go out with Lebanese chicks, Ali thought — others don't understand what it's like to be a Leb. Different when it comes to just fucking chicks; doesn't matter what they think, does it? Abdullah was going out with Mia though, being romantic and shit. She was just for him. I'd like a girlfriend too, Ali thought, but all the hot chicks I know are mates' girls or family.

The car's momentum was acutely felt by its stoned occupants. Only Mia, who wasn't stoned, was enjoying it. Abdullah appeared tense and seemed to be lacking the usual confidence this car gave him.

—You okay, babe? she asked him.

—Huh? Yeah, just freakin' out a bit. Don't want to smash up this dickhead's arse, he said, motioning with a darting finger to the car in front of them. I've had to miss two fuckin' payments on this car already, thanks to my fuckin' suspension from work.

Mia didn't know exactly why Abdullah had been suspended from his job at the railways, but she'd worked out from what he had said that it had something to do with harassment. She wasn't sure she should ask about it. The subject seemed to change his mood pretty rapidly.

Abdullah swung the car into the carpark of the Road Ripper convenience store.

—I'm goin' in ta get a drink, he said.

—Oh, get me a — Mia said, but he'd already shut the door.

She watched him walk away. He had a hot body, she mused. Worked out with weights. Needs to grow out that shaved head though. Apart from that, she wanted Abdullah Najib. She'd never wanted a guy before. There'd been cute guys, but she hadn't wanted them. She hadn't wanted to have sex with them.

—Wanna freak Abdullah out? Ali asked her.

—What do you mean?

—Ya know, freak him out when he gets back to the car.

—I guess. Depends, she said.

—Pull up that lever near the front of his seat, the one that adjusts it.

—Why?

—C'mon. Don't worry; he won't get the shits with you.

She leant over and moved the lever. Ali pushed the seat all the way forward. It looked ridiculous, because Abdullah always sat with it all the way back. They laughed. Which was good, as it cut the paranoia that hung thickly between them.

Abdullah came out of the shop with a guarana drink. He opened the door and tried to get into the seat.

—What the fuck? he snarled, but continued to force himself behind the wheel. The three passengers began to laugh.

—Ha fuckin' ha, he said, and smiled.

He released the lever and slid the seat all the way back.

—Good one, boys. Who's the fuckin' smart arse?

Ali and Fadi shut up. Mia laughed and touched Abdullah's leg

—Ooh, poor baby.

He slapped her across the jaw.

She'd never been hit. Abdullah started the car, put it in gear. If he hadn't revved the shit out of the engine and abruptly dropped the clutch, she might have thought she'd imagined it. And the slap only began to hurt once they were out on the suburban roads, which now looked sunless, harsh and a deep green. No one moved their mouths, despite the dryness.

They drove through the streets. The tension wouldn't leak out the open windows, but there was hope when the car pulled up outside Abdullah's house. At least they could escape from the scene of the incident.

—Me and Mia are just gonna go inside for a bit, Abdullah said.

Mia felt threatened, but also a little excited and even flattered that, after not saying a word since the store, he'd included her in his plans. Her mind was churning though. She got out and followed him to the door.

Ali ran his hand over his shaved head and looked at Fadi.

—Fuck. I guess we gotta stay in the fuckin' car, hey?

They laughed. Because they'd have to just sit and wait and make it seem as though they hadn't been saying anything about him when he got back. Abdullah was the undisputed leader of the guys. Partly because he had the WRX, but also because his uncle and one of his cousins were fuckin' hard cunts. Murder and shit. Abdullah had also begun to assert more lately. Since he'd been suspended without pay from his job with the railways for hassling some school girls, and since those gang bangs. Abdullah seemed to know what to do and say to get those chicks to root. It was heavy, being so forthright with the chicks, and so physical. But Abdullah's confidence seemed to make the situation flow, and they fed off each other's actions.

Abdullah motioned to Mia to sit on his bed. She moved over to it and touched it lightly.

—Hey, he began. Hey, I'm sorry, babe. You know.

He grabbed her hand. She cried, but didn't want to. It was like when she was a little girl. She'd always been able to bring on tears, tears that would get her warm, soft sympathy, or sway her father's strictness. But there were also the tears that came suddenly, and had embarrassed her, because she could tell that whoever was around — her brother, a friend or cousin — found them inappropriate. But sometimes an experience would trigger in her a deep hurt. Like hearing a baby cry for too long, or seeing a grasshopper being mobbed and eaten alive by ants. She cursed these tears because they betrayed the control she thought she had over her emotions. She knew she had good reason to cry now, but didn't want to do it here, with Abdullah. She had no idea what effect her tears would have on him.

He hugged her and kissed her neck.

—I'm sorry, babe, he said.

She hugged him back. She could feel the tension melt between them. That guy who'd smacked her in the car, that wasn't Abdullah;

this guy here was Abdullah. There was no way she would like a guy like that, a guy who'd just haul out his hard hand and smack it on her jaw. This guy here now, who felt so good, so warm and masculine, who was so confident but understanding; this was a guy she could love. He kissed her. It was so passionate. She got wet. It was so hot. He was rubbing between her legs. This was going to be it. This time she wanted it. She knew he wanted to love her. He took off her jeans. He removed his. *Jesus.* She'd never had one inside her. Not all the way inside. She wanted it. Abdullah was between her legs.

—What about a condom? she asked.

—Don't worry, babe, he said. I'll take it out at the end.

It went in. It was a shock how quickly. She'd experimented. With the handle of her hairbrush. But she'd done it slowly, millimetre by millimetre. Abdullah just popped it in, and it stung a bit. And it was so hot inside. But he stopped, and she could feel it going soft.

—Fuck, babe. I was so hot for you.

Mia sat on the toilet. The cum was dripping out. She wasn't sure if she should worry.

Abdullah was a bit pissed off that he'd come so early, but he was thinking of those sluts: you could just ram it in and blow; it didn't matter what they thought. You were never going to see them again. And they weren't going to tell your mates; your mates were there and didn't give a fuck because they were next. But anyway, Mia was in love with him. She'd let him in now. She was his.

He grabbed her around the waist as they walked back out to the car. Mia smiled at him.

★

The jets of water from the shower-rose penetrated like when she'd been sunburnt. And she washed until the soap stung. She got it all out, she thought. There was a mark on her jaw too. But she was sure Abdullah loved her now.

She'd only met Abdullah three months ago. Through Deba, a girl from school who'd invited her to a birthday party. Deba was Abdullah's cousin — or some kind of relative. Mia had liked the look of him from the first moment. The way he had control of himself. His muscles, his confidence; the way everyone around him laughed with him. And he'd kept looking over at her. Guys always looked at her, but she had wanted Abdullah's attention. Deba introduced them and he'd taken her for a drive in his car. The car did nothing for her, but he'd kissed her when he brought her back to the party. She wanted to see him every day after that, but Daddy would put an ugly end to it if he found out. He didn't like Lebanese. Peasants and terrorists, he scoffed. He didn't like any boys though, apart from Charlie. And Abdullah was always busy with his mates. They'd spent some time together, but never really alone. Once, in the back seat of his car, they'd nearly done it but then his phone had rung. She knew she wanted to sleep with him: she didn't need her virginity anymore, she'd decided. What was it for? Daddy wanted her to keep it, that was for sure, but she didn't see the point. She was the only girl in her group who hadn't done it. Even Deba, a Muslim, had done it heaps of times with her boyfriend. And it was hot, all that leading up to it. And when it went in, if he'd just done it slowly, and not pushed so hard making it sting — she could have had some more of that. It was kind of nice, what he did, but there was no way that could make her come. She'd heard sex was like that for women though. She'd once heard one of her aunties, drunk on Cinzano, telling her mother that she had to wait until her husband rolled off and fell asleep to take care of things herself. Mia did like to take care of things herself. But she'd thought that once she let Abdullah do it to her, he would have her screaming and coming all afternoon. Anyway, she'd done it now. And she was too raw from scrubbing and soap to take care of things herself.

Charlie knocked on his sister's door. It'd taken an hour and a half to work up the courage to do so. She'd looked a bit pissed off when she'd come in. Abdullah must have said something to her, about the other day, with that chick down at the old pool.

—Yeah? Mia said.

—It's me, Charlie said.

—All right.

She was putting on make-up. After a shower?

—How's it goin'? he asked.

—Not bad.

—How's Abdullah?

—Good.

—Tell ya about the other day, when I hung out with him?

—No. Why, what'd you do?

—Just hung out and that.

She either didn't know or didn't care. The former, thankfully, was more likely.

That chick had gotten away. Bolted off without her pants and started yelling. They'd left the park straight away after she'd run, rather than chase her. Thankfully. Went and had another session with the pot they'd found in the chick's jeans. Abdullah had promised Charlie that next time, next time he'd get his end in. She wasn't an Aussie anyway, Abdullah had said, and wasn't enough of a slut for all the boys to have a go. He did want to get his end in, but maybe not with a chick who's forced to do it with him. The way her voice sounded when she was running. It made him feel so sickeningly low. But Abdullah had promised that he'd get him laid. And even though the promise seemed more like a threat the more he thought about it, he had to come up with a way of getting out of receiving it. But he didn't want to tell Mia about it. How could he? Abdullah was her boyfriend. And why was Abdullah letting him see what he did to girls? It terrified Charlie that someone, who was now so close to their family, could have such alien ideas. He'd have to play along for now, he thought, because he'd rather have Abdullah think that they were friends than — what would they be if Charlie told Mia, or worse, Dad? Enemies?

—You feeling all right? he asked his sister after some silence.

—Yeah. I'll be okay, she replied.

FIFTEEN

A plank of early afternoon sun lit Sonja's face as it broke through the sheet covering Whitey's window. She had the softest breathing when she slept, like a puppy. He moved his arm from under her and kissed her forehead. She woke and smiled. He loved that smile. It was for him, and he couldn't help grinning back, and kissing her again.

—Let's go shopping, he suggested.

He bought a longneck of Coopers and they walked through the plaza close enough to smell each other. Sonja was in her school uniform and people stared. So Whitey kissed her hair. In Panties 'n' Things he bought her some bra-and-underwear sets. He let her pick them, and was impressed by her taste. In Grace Sisters he bought her a pair of Lee stretch jeans, but was asked to ditch the beer. At Fonetastic he bought her and himself pre-paid mobile phones. They had honey chicken and beef with pepper sauce at Happy Chef in the foodcourt and then went back to his flat. Sonja laughed and tossed the shopping bags aside and then lay on top of him in her new bra and jeans.

—I love you so much, Patrick, she said. I want to move in here with you.

Whitey was suddenly aware of the stubble on his chin. He felt oldish.

—Sonja, baby, I'd love that too — but what about ya mum, and ya dad?

—They can stay where they are.

—Sonja, they won't like it.

—But I like it. I want it.

—I want it too.

—I want to stay here tonight.

He hugged her and they watched TV until they fell asleep in front of Buffy, the Vampire Slayer. He woke in the still, black part of the morning and turned off the religious show that had been chasing his dreams, and knew that this daughter had now chosen him.

Sonja's eyes were something new in the morning. They were hungover from her last dream. They looked like innocence to Whitey, but also, nonchalance. Like her thoughts were anywhere but here, with him. Sonja got up to urinate.

—Good morning, baby, he croaked.

She didn't answer. She coughed and Whitey hugged her when she came out of the bathroom. There was still a lot of that dream in her eyes. She lay back down and closed them.

—Do you want coffee? he asked. Do you drink coffee?

—Mnmm.

—Okay.

He switched on the kettle and threw some powdered coffee into a couple of mugs.

—How many sugars?

—I don't know. How many do you have? I'll have the same.

Sonja sat up and wiped her mouth.

—My mum'll be freaking out, Patrick.

The front door was open as Whitey and Sonja got up to the Marmeladovs' flat. They walked in and Whitey could smell some of Sonja in the room. It was overwhelming, the familiarity and the foreignness of this place. The mother was sitting at the formica table. With two other people. Cops. Fuck. Of course. He'd seen the car outside, but this was nothing unusual for Brunei Court's carpark.

—Sonja! her mother exclaimed. My God, Sonja!

She stood, the mother, but didn't go to Sonja. She looked to Patrick White, who had just become too aware of his arms. He moved them and interlocked his fingers as the mother said something — in Russian, he supposed.

—Sonja, the female cop said, shifting her chair to engage her. Are you okay?

—Yes. I'm okay.

—Are you a relative? Or family friend? the cop asked Whitey.

—Um, yeah, a friend.

The male cop got up. And hitched his heavy belt.

—And what's your name, sir?

—Patrick. White.

—Let's just step outside, sir.

Just outside the door, which the cop closed, Whitey was already missing Sonja's smell.

—How do you know Sonja, mate?

—I'm her friend.

—How long have you known her?

—A while. A month. Or two.

—And your address?

—Here. In Brunei Court.

—Why don't we go up to your place, have a talk there.

On the way up to his flat, Whitey again felt something familiar and foreign. He'd been through this shit before with the cops. But Sonja hadn't. Should he lie? He'd never worried about lying to the cops before. Or keeping things to himself. What would Sonja keep to herself?

There was also the cold familiarity of incarceration. Or at least the familiarity of dealing with people trained to treat you as incarcerated.

They stood in his flat.

—Do you have some ID here somewhere, mate?

—Yeah. Licence.

—What happened to Sonja last night?

—She was with me.

—Do you know her mother was unaware of Sonja staying out last night?

—No. Well yeah, I guess.

—Are you having a relationship with Sonja?

—I guess.

—Sexual?

—I'm her boyfriend.

—And how old do you believe Sonja to be?

—She's a teenager.

—Yes, she's a teenager. And you're how old, sir?

Whitey looked at his sink. With the two coffee cups in it. He didn't answer.

—I'll just have to check your ID down at the car, mate. Stay here for a while, okay, we'll come and have a word with you shortly.

The flat was raw. Concrete walls. Sink. It smelt only of himself. Sonja had taken her scent home with her. Whitey smoked a few cigarettes. Drank tap water. Both cops came back, and told him that Sonja and her mother had decided to leave things the way they were now, with Sonja staying at her mother's place. Whitey was not to go over there and to avoid any further contact with the Marmeladovs. No charges would be pressed. The constables were aware that Patrick White had recently done some time.

—It would be a good idea to stay well away, the male cop advised him. The girl could get you into trouble.

Whitey went out for a walk. There was too much of that imprisoned feeling growing. You learn to live basically when you're in prison. You take some solace in it. But this was complex. A complex stripping of liberties. Nevertheless, it brought back his sentence. He'd been able to not think about it, to move forward. Because of Sonja. But now it came flooding back.

You have the basics in jail. Water. Shelter. Food. Company. The taps are like outdoor domestic ones. But stronger, and unbreakable by hand. And the water tastes like a garden tap's: tinny — flavoured by the corroding pipes. The thick walls only let in a faint, filtered figment of the elements. And though removed of choice and taste, the food was looked forward to. And you could talk. And bullshit. Or confess. Or listen, and try to work out what was bullshit. Whitey had tried, in his first few weeks inside, to think that things could be worse. He could have been destitute, or dying slowly and painfully. But it was best not to look for comparisons. Or to think too much about anything. Especially time. The way he'd been made to pay. It was an experience that would one day be over — gone with the accompanying slice of his life. Things could only be worse if he was serving more time, like most of the other guys in there. So he kept this thought to himself and watched the other guys, without looking, or being seen to look. Whitey was thankfully excused, because of his short term there, from the bulk of the politics. There were networks of hatred. Allies. Dogs. Cunts. But they did all live together. Mostly the hatred just simmered. And mostly it was misdirected. True enemies existed outside the walls of H Block.

These bricks of memory began to mesh and set with the present. So he walked and tried to direct his mind into another stream. He hadn't drunk or smoked pot or had any speed while in jail. He hadn't really missed it either. There were drugs in there, but Whitey couldn't afford them, and no one had offered to blow him out. He'd have to be careful now, if he was going to play along with this new imprisonment, as he'd be under surveillance now. Sonja's gone. Drugs'll have to go, for a while, he thought. Or I'll have to move. Because the cops, he knew, wouldn't look away for long this time.

He did want Sonja though. And really, he was prepared to defy law and family to be with her. It all depended on her.

They both cried when she turned up later that afternoon. They cried and hugged in the kitchenette. Until Whitey broke from her, and wiped his face with his T-shirt.

—So, he said.

—I'm going to stay here, with you.

—The cops'll come and get you.

—My mum won't call them. She hates them. They weren't very nice to her before we got there this morning. She hates them anyway. So does my dad. They always have, I think. She says I made her desperate though. Now she knows where I am, she won't call them.

—What did your dad say?

—He doesn't know. Mum isn't going to tell him. Until he's better. Until he comes home.

—So you're mum's just letting you?

—Well, I won't be seeing her anymore.

—What do you mean?

—She said to make a choice. If I thought I was old enough to have a boyfriend, I was old enough to make a choice. Between her and you. And I'm here, Patrick.

—Fuck.

—That wasn't the reaction I was hoping for, she said.

—No. No, not a bad fuck, I mean, you know, it's heavy, but I love you. You know.

—So. Can I stay?

They hugged and kissed and had sex in the kitchenette, Whitey pulling her close to get her scent on him. Because each inward breath that caught her scent excluded everything in the world but her, and his immediacy with her.

After, they lay on his mattress, Sonja with her head on Whitey's chest. Home and Away was on, but it was just providing a perfect half-light.

—What about your family, Patrick, you've never mentioned any of them once. Tell me about them.

—I don't talk to 'em. Well, haven't for years. I think maybe we don't care for each other, at least not the way your family cares about you.

—Tell me why.

Whitey's dad had been a long-haul truck-driver. Sydney to Melbourne, Sydney to Cobar, Sydney to Brisbane. Sydney to anywhere on the eastern side of Australia — some of the destinations sounded more like they were in Africa, or India. Whitey knew the names of places even his primary school teachers hadn't heard of. It was cool when his dad would bring one of the rigs home. The cabin — it wasn't anything like a car up there; it was like the control room from that show on the telly, Time Tunnel. And the dog-box in the back — Whitey had asked if they could put one on the side of the house and he'd have it as his bedroom. He'd gone on a couple of trips with his dad, but it was really only exciting for the first few hours; then Whitey would wish he was back at home, out in the yard, or riding his beat-up old BMX. His dad would wish Whitey was back at home too.

—Ya doin' me head in with that bloody moanin', kid. Put a sock in it, hey.

But really, Whitey didn't see much of his dad other than when he'd come home for a few days every couple of months. And the house would change when he was there. Whitey would be shocked to see this man, his dad, walk out of his mum's bedroom, or out of the toilet. And Whitey and his little sister would lose their mum while Dad was there. Instead of being the mother, she'd be more like another child — playing up to Dad, acting a bit silly, giggling, and spending too long in the bedroom with him. But then his dad would leave again, for Gunnedah, or the Glasshouse Mountains, and Whitey's mum was back for him and his sister.

He couldn't remember ever really getting in trouble from his mum. Couple of times for letting the dog maul the towels on the line or for teasing his sister. But life was calm and uncomplicated until that morning; or maybe it just seemed that way looking back because of how everything slid into a different world from then on.

His mum had just gotten them up for school. Whitey was in the toilet, and hadn't even heard the phone ring. But he heard his mum scream. Or howl. And he knew. He was only ten. But he knew. Dad was dead. Killed flying down the highway in his time tunnel.

His mum had held it together at the funeral, at which Whitey and his sister had had to wear clothes borrowed from the neighbours, and he was surprised because seeing the coffin — his big dad in that small box — made him spurt out sobs where he hadn't felt the need to cry at all until then. But really, from the moment they got back home after the strange party at his auntie's house, Whitey's mum was changed. The fussiness over every little grain of dust that used to drive him nuts dissipated. And the mash potatoes were watery, or were really just that: mashed potatoes — no milk, no butter, no salt. And sometimes it was just Weet-Bix for dinner. And then, a few months after the funeral, the migraines. His mum would be crawling — like that chameleon lizard he'd seen on telly — down the hallway, and vomiting and groaning in a voice so low it was like a man's. And then she'd be in bed. And she wouldn't move or answer when they'd ask if she was okay.

But one day she got a job at the doctor's as a receptionist. She was there at home when they went to school, but she wouldn't get home until after eight in the evenings. She'd never taught Whitey to cook, but he'd had to learn. And he learnt pretty quickly, although he couldn't manage more than one thing at a time. So they'd have sausages or mash potatoes, or chops or chips. One night Whitey burned the frozen shepherd's pie to a cinder, so he and his sister had a cup of white sugar each for dinner.

By the time he was in high school, his younger-by-six-years sister was starting to give him the shits. She was so clingy. He had to cook, listen to her talk about this and that girl at school, and explain every little thing about everything they were watching on the telly. Sometimes he'd just take off on his bike, cruise around, and go lie on the cool grass up at the local sports oval.

Soon he was meeting up with kids from school and smoking pot with them, and not long after he got a job at Hedda's café cleaning up after the old ladies, and was able to buy enough pot to sell. He moved out of home one night without telling either his mother or sister. He slept on people's lounges or on mates' bedroom floors. He knew, even back then, that it was a cowardly thing to just piss off like that, but time soon filled in the feeling with a numbness, and it was two years before he had any contact with his mother or sister.

It was his sister's birthday. It was a date he always remembered, so he turned up at the house. It was as if they were expecting him. They didn't act surprised at all. Just said hi, let him in. They were having a barbecue, some of his sister's school friends were there, and Whitey offered to cook. Towards the end of the last batch of snags his sister came up to him.

—Happy birthday, he said.

—Thanks.

—I didn't bring you a present. Sorry.

—Thought not.

Whitey hadn't even thought of a present, until he'd seen that there was a table with several gift-wrapped CDs and books.

—I think I've got some money if you want.

He had a single ten in his pocket, which she took.

And when he was leaving — he would have to walk, as he now had no bus fare — his mother grabbed his forearm.

—We knew you weren't dead. We're just waitin' for the call though.

Whitey didn't know what to feel after that. They were his family, but he treated them, and they treated him, like a former neighbour or less. That was the last time he'd seen them. He'd wondered, while in jail, if they knew he was there. But he hadn't even thought of them until now. Until Sonja had asked him.

He held Sonja, and hoped that she'd never leave him the way he'd left his family.

SIXTEEN

Dad's a fuckin' loser, Abdullah thought. Lives by all those rules; rules that don't apply to life. Like the religion. All that devotion. Devotion to things outside your life. Putting things first, things you can't see or grab hold of. And all those rules at work. Keeping your mouth shut. Dealing with cunts all day. And Aussie bosses telling you about policies and that shit. Dad loves all that shit. And expects me to too. Disappointed in me, his own fuckin' son. He's the one who told us how, when he first came to Australia, the Aussies would spit on him at the bus stop, and the factory bosses would tell him they don't employ bloody Arabs. Well, he can have the fuckin' railways. And Allah. My cousins are the fuckin' lucky ones in my family. Their parents realise how wrong all these big-headed arseholes and sluts are. Mum and Dad say we're all lucky to be here, things are good here. Dad puts up with it. The Aussies looking down on him, sweeping their crap up off the station. Not Abdullah. I'm going to be like my cousins and uncle, he thought, as he drove to their house to have a smoke with his cousin Yift. No Aussies are going to look down their stubby noses at me, no sluts are going to laugh at me, tell me there's no way they'd touch a Leb.

Abdullah was born in Australia. As was his sister three years later. His parents had emigrated as refugees, with Yift's parents, in the 1970s after their whole town collapsed from Israeli shelling. Abdullah's father had told him how he and his brothers had helped the Hezbollah — clearing the roads for them, feeding them and giving them water. And how he'd seen corpses left like animal pelts to evaporate in the sun. How he'd seen a friend of his from the town, dragging his severed leg by a still-attached rope of flesh. Abdullah loved to hear the stories. But his father was sparse with them. So was his uncle. But where his father had left war behind for good, Abdullah's uncle had identified the war going on here, in this shithole country. Not a blatant war with ordnance and jet-bombers, but one where the Aussies, like the Jews, had all the backing, and the Lebs were the freedom-fighters. The Aussies had the pigs and the politicians on their side, but the Lebs had the courage, and the history of war. The Aussies tried to keep you down with their rules and laws suited to their backward Christian ways; made you talk all English with a stupid skip accent, made you stay in school and learn their stupid Abo history, and the blondie, tarted-up girls avoided or just laughed at you. Abdullah's uncle and cousin had both done time. Attempted murder and possession with intent to sell. They never talked about it. Abdullah didn't know the whole story. But it impressed him, and it impressed his mates even more.

Back when he was a little kid, Abdullah and his sister had attended a primary school in the western suburbs because his mother was a cleaner there. His cousins and all his friends had gone to school in the area they lived in, in the Arabic precinct of Punchbowl in south-western Sydney. Abdullah and his sister were the only Lebanese kids in their school. There were some Turks, but they were Christians, and snobs. There were a couple of boys that Abdullah made friends with,

David and Thomas, but, although they were friendly, they were also bookish, and would talk about things Abdullah would get lost in, like some stupid novel they were reading, or that dragons and dragons game or whatever it was, and they'd laugh when he'd try to chip in on a conversation. Eventually they became enemies, like everyone else there, after he jobbed David for teasing him about his bum-fluff moustache that was starting to grow.

Abdullah could handle the boys — they were all scared of him by Year 4 — but the girls baffled him. They'd giggle and flitter around David and Thomas and the other boys, but avoid even eye contact with Abdullah. Some days they'd be hysterically laughing and falling about each other at recess, but then crying their eyes out at lunch. Abdullah's sister, his cousins, none of the girls from his area were like that. They were quiet and gentle, and he never saw them display their emotions as though they were actors on a soap opera; and never engaged in the games with boys that these girls did. There were two he really liked though: Jillian and Liz. Jillian had thick, dark hair, and her dark eyes were even darker because of her milky skin. Liz was blonde, and all the boys liked her. The girls never talked to him, and often moved when he sat next to them. One lunchtime though, when he was in Year 6, Abdullah's sister came to him and told him that Alison, the little sister of one of the girls in Abdullah's class, had told her that Liz had a crush on him, and if he asked her out, she'd go with him. Abdullah thought about nothing else for the rest of the week. And over the weekend convinced himself to ask her out. On Monday at recess, he went up to Liz where she was sitting on the benches outside the girls' toilets with her friends.

—Can I talk to ya? he asked her.
—Um, why? she said.

—Just wanna aks ya something.

She laughed, but said —Well, go, I'm not stopping you.

—Um, would you like to go out with me?

—Go out? With you?

—Yeah.

—Yuck! She burst into laughter, and her friends followed. Other kids heard and scuffed over to see what was so funny.

—But my sister told me you liked me, he whined, anger and nausea boiling up in him.

—Your sister's a woggy freak like you. As if. Keep away. Please, Liz said, and the swelling group laughed, and Abdullah just wanted to cut sick and thrash out with arms and legs and make pies out of their stupid skip heads. But he went up to the back of the sports oval and sat with his back against the football posts. He found out later that week that it had been a set-up. And he'd gone for it like the dog they thought he was.

He hated Liz then. He just wanted to bash her. She was ugly. And fake. And a slut for all her Aussie boys. Jillian he fell more in love with. But he would never talk to her. He would never talk to any of the bitches here. But he would fantasise. He'd dream of getting Jillian alone. Just the two of them. Lifting her skirt. Seeing her undies. Pushing her down. Lying on top of her. Pinning her down. Making her love him for his strength. And then leaving her half-naked, or fully naked, and letting everyone see her how she was. Weak and small, and defenceless without her confidence he'd so easily overcome. And she would want him. Because no one else would like her. But back in the reality of Plumpton Primary, everyone loved Jillian and hated Abdullah — whispering and snickering and carrying on in that language and manner that had always eluded him.

But then thankfully Year 6 was over and he was at high school. Punchbowl Boys' High. Back with his boys. He felt tough. He'd started to fill out a bit. And his uncle was in prison. He was one of the main boys at the school. Kids wanted to hang out with him. They wanted to know what it was like at the skip school, out there with all the sluts in miniskirts. They wanted to hear it so he told them. How many fucks he got. How they all fucked out there. Their parents let them do anything, he told them, they fuck in the dunnies, in the drains behind the school, anywhere you wanted. And they deserved it. Flashing everything. Legs, tits. No shame, no pride, nothing like Muslim girls. And it became legend. It became truth. Those miserable, isolating years out there had paid off. He was able to construct an experience that reversed, he thought, their impact on him. It became so true that even one of the dumb skip teachers at Punchbowl Boys took him aside and asked him why he boasted about that sort of thing. Abdullah laughed.

—Where's your daughter go to school, sir? he taunted the teacher. If it wasn't for the principal being a Leb, he thought, he would have gotten suspended.

High school was good. There were no girls, but that was an advantage. You could be yourself. No bitches around to laugh at you, make you feel stupid. And Abdullah was respected. Amongst boys, Arabic boys, what he said was funny when he meant it to be, tough when he meant it to be, and his ideas were valued. There were a couple of groups who didn't like him and his boys — the dickheads who got into studying, were full-on into the religion, who played skip-ball, or were too wimpy to stand up for themselves and were happy to become Aussies. But Abdullah's gang, although small in number, were undisputed as the toughest.

Where it was just talk in the early years of high school, Abdullah and his boys all shared the intensity of their frustration by the last two years. At home, there was no talking about sex. But at school, and hanging out after school at the pinnie joint, or at Bankstown Mall, it was the whole world. Abdullah was the core, and all talk would gravitate to him — because he'd had so many bitches, knew what it was like to hold a girl, and put his cock right up in her. He could easily imagine what it would be like, he thought, so the stories came easily to him.

In fact, he shared his mates' frustration and confusion. The only girl he really knew was his sister. And she was into mosque and the Koran and gave him absolutely no clue into the psyche of what girls thought about when it came to sex. And he could never ask. That would be one thing his parents would go to war about. One time his father had severely beaten him when he found a copy of *Barely Legal* behind the bed-head. So the stories stayed stories. But turned to plans. How were they going to get laid? Sure, you meet a Muslim girl, and if you're lucky she'll let you get a taste before the wedding, but what do you do now? There's so much horny pussy out there, and a man needs to be a man.

Abdullah left Punchbowl Boys at the end of Year 11. He wasn't doing well at school, and his dad had gotten him an interview at the railways. The interview was piss-easy, Abdullah thought, walking out of the office — three Lebs whom his father had had 'round for dinner a few times. He started a month later at Macdonaldtown Station, collecting tickets and sweeping up the platform. The job was a bludge, and there were plenty of hot chicks from the performing arts high school in the morning and afternoons. He was also able to get a car loan, and bought the 2001 WRX, fully worked and detailed. The freedom fight was fully under way. Man, the chicks really paid attention when they heard the turbo! And he'd begun to look better in the mirror. Working out. Shaving his head. Buying cool clothes. Tight white T-shirts and Hugo Boss jeans. But then the cops. Twice in one week pulled him up for speeding. Hassled the fuck out of him, searched his car, searched him, and made him wait while they checked for non-existent warrants. Asked him at least three times if he was Lebanese. Fuckin' arsehole skips. And then, just a week later: he'd started to notice a group of girls from the performing arts school smile at him. One was hot. Really hot. Long, curly black hair. And her skirt sitting nice and high on her thighs. She never had her student ticket with her, so one morning late that week after the cops had hassled him, he waited. When she was coming through the turnstile he locked it.

—Ticket please.

—Um, I left it at home, she said.

—That's too bad, miss, you'll have to go home and get it, he winked at her.

—You're kidding, right. I've got to get to school. I have a composition exam this morning.

—We'll, maybe we can work something out then, he said, and unlocked the turnstile for a second, and then re-locked it, smiling at her.

—Look, mister, are you going to let me through or not?

—Depends, honey. What's your name?

—Princesse de bloody Lascabanes.

—Princess, hey?

—Are you going to let me through?

—For a kiss.

Abdullah leant down to her. But she jumped the barrier, so he grabbed her hard on the arse. She screamed and ran off with her friends who'd been waiting for her. There'd also been, Abdullah suddenly noticed, quite a few other passengers waiting to get through the turnstile.

The railways suspended him, without pay, until they completed their investigation. What a load of fuckin' shit, he thought. Well, fuck them.

—Abdullah, you muthafucka, his cousin Yift said, coming into the lounge room. Let's get fuckin' goin', huh?

—What took ya so long? Puttin' on ya fuckin' make-up? Abdullah taunted, and winked at Sakine, Yift's little sister.

They put ciggies in their mouths and lit them as they crossed the threshold of the screen-door. They smoked them in silence before getting in the car. Abdullah liked this: it showed that his cousin had respect for him — not smoking in the car — and as Yift was the person he probably respected most in the world, apart from his uncle, Yift's father; this was a big thing.

—Did I tell ya I'm fuckin' a cop's daughter? Abdullah said.

—Nuh. What are ya doin' that for? Cops are fuckwits, mate.

—She's not a fuckin' cop. Her father, mate.

—You're a fuckin' idiot, mate. You can fuck yaself up. Fuckin' cop; don't get involved with those cunts. Me and me dad have fuckin' done time, and you're fuckin' cops. Disrespectful, ya dickhead.

This wasn't the reaction Abdullah had hoped for. He was hurt. But wouldn't show it. He loved his cousin and his uncle. He'd adopted them as brother and father. And he thought that he'd been adopted too, as a brother and a son. But this reaction made him feel he was back at Plumpton Primary — on his own, unable to understand why, what was fully formed and perfect in his mind was so wrong to others. Couldn't Yift see? This girl was an advantage; fucking with the enemy. He thought Yift would love it. It's like taking a prisoner, or something.

—Let's get whacked, Yift said.

Yift smoked the gear until the bowl was clean and then said he wanted to go home. He didn't talk at all for the duration of the session. Just packed the cones. Smoked one, offered one, smoked one, offered one. But Abdullah only had three. He wasn't in the mood. He'd wanted to tell Yift about the sluts he and his boys had been getting. Get him in on the next one. Show him that he'd started out on his own with his gang. Started something mad. Yift didn't want to talk though. Just packed and smoked. And looked out the window on the way back to his place.

—Take it easy, mate, he mumbled, as he shut the passenger door of the WRX.

Abdullah called Mia on her mobile. He needed to gauge what he was doing with her. He was doubting and needed to shift blame. He'd thought that telling Yift about her would build something. He'd imagined a handshake and some long laughter and hard shoulder-punching. But here he was. With Mia as his girlfriend, but wondering what her worth to him was.

—Hello, she said.

—Hey, Mia. What're ya doin'?

—Not much. What are you doing?

—Fuck all. Can I pick you up? Go for a root or something.

—Abdullah. Don't talk to me like that please. Look, I don't know. My dad will freak if I ask him if I can go out. And also, we need to get condoms if we're going to do that again.

—Huh? Well, what's ya brother doin'? Does he wanna hang out?

—My brother? What do you mean?

—Just ask him if he wants to hang out.

—All right. Hang on.

He could hear her talking, but not what she was saying. It pissed him off.

—Yeah, he wants to hang out, she replied. He'll wait for you out the front of our place.

Between eight and nine pm on late-night shopping nights, the fever of teenage behaviour changed Rooty Hill Plaza. It became a meeting place, and more importantly, it became a blueing place, and a pick-up place. The families and older couples were forced out by the swearing and spitting and tiny denim skirts, and were lined up to pay for their parking by eight o'clock.

Abdullah and Charlie hung at the top of the escalators. They'd headed out west again in the WRX because, Abdullah insisted, this was where the sluts really were.

—Hey, babe, Abdullah called out to all the girls who came up the hungry metal stairs. Most of them rolled their eyes, told him to shut up, dickhead. There were also plenty of westie guys around, and as Abdullah had little faith in Charlie's abilities as a half-decent bluer, he'd have to be a little bit careful. Sly.

—Hey, babe.

—Hey, a chick with blue eye-shadow said. What're youse doin'?

—Just hangin'? What're you girls doin'?

—Same.

—Smoke pot? Abdullah asked, and shifted his hand on the banister so it bumped Charlie's. There were two of them. Both Aussie, and both pretty hot.

—Sometimes.

—What about tonight?

—Why? Ya got some?

—Of course, babe.

Abdullah called Fadi on one of the chicks' mobile phones. It was one of the new Nokias. He'd be keeping it too; put his own SIM card in it.

—Fadi. It's Abdullah. I'm usin' a slut's phone. Can ya get ya dad's car?

—Maybe. Why, what's up, mate?

—Mate, sluts, sluts. We got sluts down at Brownthistle Park at Mt Druitt. They wanna suck ya dick.

These guys had seemed okay. A bit woggish, and the older one a bit cocky, but pretty cool and undemonstrative; and willing to blow them out when it seemed that no one had any pot at all. Tennille Baxter had reasoned that it would be okay to go for a ride with them up to the oval for a smoke. But after that first wrong turn, and then him locking the car doors and telling them to shut the fuck up, things had gone from something just a little out of the ordinary to something that was quite sharply threatening — something with potential teeth, but which she'd never thought she'd have to try to placate. She and Melissa had gone for plenty of smokes with boys before. But none had acted anything like this. A joint had been passed around, but the locked doors, and the total silence of the younger guy had stripped the mood entirely, leaving only unwanted paranoia. And then, as if he thought he was in a porno or something, the older guy said:

—So, do you girls wanna fuck or what?

Tennille wasn't sure what to say. Or do. But she was quite aware that there were two guys here, both much bigger and stronger than she and Melissa, and they didn't intend to just smoke a joint and take them home, like they'd said. Melissa was silent. Her posture was one of total fear: her hands between her legs, her body a nervous shell. But Tennille was still acutely aware. They could get out of this. They could survive this. She remembered a novel she'd read in high school, an autobiography, about a young woman who'd been raped. Despite her fear and disgust, the woman had done what the sick bastard had asked her to do, and she'd lived through it — where other victims had not. The absolute last thing Tennille wanted to do was have sex with these guys. But she didn't want to die. *Jesus.* Not now, like this. While the threat was still just words, she thought she would try reason first.

—Look, we don't fuck, okay?

—Why'd youse come then?

—We thought, you know, you'd give us a smoke.

—Have a fuckin' smoke then.

—No, thanks. I think we'll just go now.

—Uh-uh. You're here with us now. Let's have a bit of fun, hey.

—No. Please, we just want to go.

—Hey, you got us all horny. Now I think we should fuck, okay.

The guy had turned almost fully around in his seat and was looking into her. He'd started to raise his voice. Tennille shrank back. She couldn't think of anything else to say. He was slicing back at her with a response to everything she said.

—You ready? he asked, his eyes wide now.

—We can't fuck you. We have boyfriends.

—Boyfriends? If you fuck them, you can fuck us, right?

—No, please.

—All right. Look. Ya startin' ta piss me off now. How about you just come over here with me and suck me off, and your friend here gets with my mate?

—We can't fuck youse though.

—Just a suck, baby.

Melissa looked at her now, her eyes wide with accusations of betrayal. Tennille quickly shrugged and shook her head once. She could see no other way. To refuse would prolong this, and make it more violent than just this guy's foul mouth.

—Give us your mobile, the guy barked at her. She found it in her bag and handed it to him.

—Nice one, he said. He got out of the car and called someone. She couldn't hear what he was saying, but he was laughing. What a fucking arsehole. He got back in and winked at his mate. Then the younger guy took Melissa and stood outside the car. Tennille had to crawl through to the front seats then and sit in the passenger seat. He undid his jeans and pulled his jocks down and exposed his cock. It wasn't big, and it wasn't hard, and it was ugly, and where every other time the sight of one in the flesh had aroused her, this was something else: this was an animal's thing.

—Suck it, bitch.

She went to it. This was the most repulsive, degrading thing she'd ever done. She would have rather eaten dirt for a year than do this. There was nothing sexy in this. She'd done it before, but it was different, it had tasted like something new and exciting: this was nauseating and totally invasive and she could taste every filthy cell of sweat and piss. She knew enough from the last time she'd done this, of her own free will, and as soon as she felt it spasm, she withdrew her head and got out of the way. He spurted all over himself and his seat.

—They're Recaros, bitch, he said, and slapped her on the neck.

Melissa and the young guy now got back in the car. Tennille could hear what was going on, and was relieved when it seemed like the guy had shot out of the starting-blocks before his race began. Then a car pulled up right next to them. They'll let us go for sure now, she thought, they won't want to be seen doing this. But the guy she'd had to take in her mouth got out and was shaking hands with these guys. He knew them. They were his mates. Another guy got in the seat next to her.

—So, what about a fuck then? he said.

—No. Look, I already told your mate, just one head job, and that's it.

—Nah, a fuck I think, the guy urged, and showed her the pistol.

SEVENTEEN

Salvatore Testafiglia ended the telephone conversation with his mother and replaced the receiver. She'd told him, finally, why his sister and brother-in-law had been absent from all the family occasions for the past ten years. Salvatore had thought his brother-in-law avoided them because he was Napoletano; too good for his wife's Calabrese family. That's what his parents had told him. But no, his mother now said, it was because his brother-in-law wanted nothing to do with a family where incest was ignored or swept away. Because, as Salvatore had just learnt, his father had abused Mary, Salvatore's sister, on and off for twelve years of their shared youth.

Ten years ago, Mary had told her husband about her childhood. And now, he'd finally convinced her to seek counselling. One of the things she'd decided to do in seeking help was, despite her father being dead, to report the crime to the police. His mother was talking of all this now because she assumed he'd hear about it, being a police officer. Naivety with regard to probity in the police force sparked in him a pang of almost hatred through him. But he had to remind himself that where she came from, secrets are not something private but simply fodder for gossip.

My father, Salvatore thought, did that? His blood is flowing through me?

Salvatore was older than Mary. He loved her, but the family dynamic also came into play. Salvatore loved his mother, because she loved him. Salvatore's father loved his daughter. And was hard on Salvatore. He had harboured some resentment, and jealousy, toward his sister because of this. The smell of his father's tobacco and grappa breath, his tough brown hands, and the look, as though he knew something about you; something you'd forgotten, but something bad. And this little doll: Salvatore's sister.

The family respected Giuseppe Testafiglia. It was their family's culture. But sometimes Salvatore had wished his father would die. Life was smooth and happy at home when it was just Salvatore, his mother and sister. But when his father came home from work things could turn harsh and unpredictable. Everything had to be the way his father liked it. But his preferences could change from day to day, and cause a solid whack on the back of Salvatore's head. Some days his father would want to hear about Salvatore's day at school, and he'd have to stand in the lounge room and carefully detail the day's events. Other days Salvatore would have to be totally silent, and not even cause the floorboards to squeak. Salvatore would fantasise about his father falling from one of the houses he built in the suburbs. Smashing his concrete-splashed ute on the way home. And there was that time he asked his sister — really just to cruelly tease her, because he thought she loved their father, because of the special way he treated her — if she ever wished the father dead and she said yes. It was clear now why his father gave Mary special treatment and the sickness of it burned inside Salvatore.

Mary had eloped. Went to live with her new parents-in-law. And Salvatore's father got the heart problems. Then couldn't understand why his son wanted to become a *poliziotto* — what practical use was a policeman to the family? But Salvatore paid no heed, and became a police officer. The rules, enforcement; it was far more practical than his father could know. He respected his job — and received respect. And he'd figured out how to live in this country; something his father never really worked out. His father never properly learnt English, and was constantly in conflict with people and organisations over what were usually simple misunderstandings. Salvatore thought he'd been successful; successful in growing into someone who did not resemble his father.

His father was dead by the time Salvatore got married. Everything that upset the father caused damage to his heart and killed him a little — he made it family lore — but it was lung cancer complications that finally finished him. Two months from diagnosis to a small, grey dead thing on the bed. Salvatore took his new wife to visit the grave when it'd been there for nearly two years.

He'd met Maria at the Carciofo Club in the western suburb of Wetherill Park, which was then only metres away from orchards and chicken farms and, ironically, Anglo-Saxon heartland. She was with her brothers and cousins. They were all there for the *barzalleta* and the *canzone*, told and sung by people who know the ironies concerning Italians in Australia. Her parents liked Salvatore's quiet, polite way, and he became a part of Maria's family. He was surprised, and a little turned off by Maria's keenness to become his lover. He was, of course, always aroused when they were intimate with each other, but he had intended not to sleep with her until they were married. Her desires shocked him, and he even considered that maybe they weren't right for each other after she told him she'd done it before, with her ex-boyfriend — a guy Salvatore knew from church. The extent of Salvatore's experience was limited to the kissing and touching he'd done with her. But after Maria eventually got him to follow his desire all the way, he, of course, forgot about his resolve to save it for the wedding night; and they soon got married at St Joseph's in Leichhardt as intended.

He and Maria had a child, and their daughter absolved anything that was imperfect in his life. Artemesia, Mia, smelt like life; she was alive, lively but precious. Salvatore was devoted. And a few years after the birth of their son he found, like his father, that he was devoted to his daughter more than his son. But he loved his son because he was a son. And proved to be a good child. But not inspiring like his firstborn. Because everything Salvatore did — his work, his responsibilities at home — he did with Mia in mind. He could not remember what had driven him prior to Mia's birth.

Salvatore could think of no greater hell than his daughter hating him eternally. He'd have to try and improve his relationship with her. She was becoming an adult, like his sister. Who hated her father, and would always hate him. Salvatore had never done, would never do, what his father had done. But knowing this had planted the thought in him — the thought that he would have to improve his relationship with Mia. But how? He was being a good father, wasn't he? Not just providing for her, but ensuring she had a safe life, and instilling values that he knew were correct. Could he allow her some more freedom? Could he trust her to be honest with him if he did? It was intensely painful to Salvatore that he didn't know how he could keep the love of his little girl. But he would have to. Whatever the answer may be, he would have to.

It was easy to preoccupy himself with other concerns though; he had solutions or at least policies for other people's problems.

★

Salvatore took the files that had been cluttering up his desk out to the clerical officer and placed them on her workstation.

—These are the files I requested you take out of my office last week.

—Not a problem, she said, not looking at him.

He returned to his office, shaking his head as Sergeant Rosales came down the narrow corridor trying to attract his attention by waving a newspaper at him.

—One of the girls has talked to the paper, Sal, Sergeant Rosales said, catching the Senior Sergeant in the office doorway and handing him the tabloid paper.

—Shit, Salvatore said, folding the copy of the *Telegraph Post* to focus on the single column. All right, he continued, folding the paper the other way. One of the girls identified someone, didn't she? Sold her drugs before the rape?

—Yeah. Should we talk to him? Tell the media liaison department we've got someone helping us with our inquiries?

—Yes. Get him down here. We'll talk to him. You and I.

Senior Sergeant Testafiglia wanted to see Patrick White immediately, but it was crucial to make a suspect wait. No matter who they are, if you make them wait, they're more likely to tell the truth. Some cops believe that giving a suspect too much time to think before questioning gives them an opportunity to cook up well-constructed lies. But Salvatore knew the opposite to be true. The longer they are made to wait, the more they feel the gravity; the more they want to escape the atmosphere they're in. They're relieved to see you finally walk through the door, pleased to help you in order to help themselves.

Finally, he opened the door and let Sergeant Rosales enter before himself. They both sat and opened files.

—So, he began. We like drugs and young women do we?

—Sorry? Patrick White replied.

—Done some time for possession, haven't you?

—Yeah.

—And you have a thing for young women.

—My girlfriend is younger than me, yeah.

—Are they all your girlfriends?

—Are who? Patrick White replied.

—Do you know a Natalie Caxaro?

—Natalie. Yeah I know Nat. Why, what's happened to Nat?

—Can you tell us what happened the last time you saw her?

—She came around to — she came around and we hung out for a bit. Not for long though. Five minutes, not even. Why?

—Smoke some weed? Senior Sergeant Testafiglia suggested, and took off his glasses.

—Nuh.

—Tell some of ya mates where they could catch up with her in an inebriated state?

—What? What mates?

—Some of the boys you sell to. Middle Eastern boys. Some of your Leb mates?

—Leb mates? I think ya talkin' ta the wrong bloke.

—And what about this young girl you're carrying on with? Senior Sergeant Testafiglia continued, and flicked through some handwritten notes. Sonja.

—She's a friend.

—There's been some trouble though. Police have talked to you already. The young constable who brought you in told me Sonja was there at your flat this morning.

—Yeah. It's cool though.

—Oh. Oh, it's cool is it? Was it cool with Natalie, was it? She doesn't think it was very cool.

—What? What do you mean? Maybe she's jealous, Patrick White offered, and looked over to Sergeant Rosales, because he was lost; both cops could tell.

—We're going to talk to a couple of other people, and keep you here until we sort some things out, Senior Sergeant Testafiglia concluded.

Salvatore Testafiglia knew when people were lying. There had been only a few whose talent had exceeded his of detecting the truth. This Patrick White had done time. He could be a good liar. It's a defence mechanism some men have to use to survive in jail. But beyond knowing one of the victims, and possibly dealing drugs again, there was little else. Senior Sergeant Testafiglia had told the media liaison department that they had someone. No name yet though. The young girls and their parents would have to be talked to. A charge could be laid yet if Patrick White was breaching any of his parole conditions. And the press would continue to draw long bows. The actual perpetrators were still to be identified, but proactive police work reported in the media kept the bosses happy.

Before heating up his lunch he went to tell Patrick White what his immediate future held for him.

—There's just the matter of sorting out what was going on this morning with the young girl you're not meant to have any contact with. So if there's anyone you need to call, work maybe, we'll make that possible for you. You could be here for a while.

—No. That's okay. Thanks.

—Some advice, mate: young women quite often have parents who will do anything to keep them away from guys. If a girl's parents don't like you, steer clear.

—Yeah, okay.

—Take the advice. Once this is sorted.

Senior Sergeant Testafiglia dispensed this fatherly wisdom despite knowing that it was unlikely to be taken. Although he lacked some of the cockiness, this guy was typical, he thought, of the Anglo-Australians out here in the western suburbs. The lazy, nonchalant manner, the apparent lack of drive to change the negative things impinging on their lives. Sure, he'd accepted the advice, but it was just so he could escape this immediate situation. Senior Sergeant Testafiglia knew that no matter what he said to this guy, it would not go on to influence any aspect of his life once he got out of here. He doubted whether even his prison time had changed him. Because Salvatore knew the type. These Anglo-Aussies and their atheistic, existential way of life. Family scattered all over. No structure. Teenagers living out on their own. And just taking each day as it comes. A freedom that seemed regressive to Senior Sergeant Testafiglia. Sometimes he felt an overwhelming urge to literally hammer some sense into these people who came through his branch of the legal system.

EIGHTEEN

Sonja had been missing a lot of school. She wondered if they'd written a letter to her parents yet. The principal had been a bit sus when Sonja had been sent to her for not wearing a uniform. Sonja told her that she'd ripped it and that her parents couldn't afford a new one. The principal had called Sonja's mother but had obviously been hung up on. She'd given Sonja a second-hand uniform from lost property.

Sonja would be missing school altogether today. How could she go now? The police had just come and taken Patrick. No explanation other than that he was required to attend the station. And then they'd asked her what she was doing there, in his flat. Patrick had interrupted them though, and said he'd go with them — said he wanted to sort out whatever it was as soon as possible. So they'd taken him. She'd have to go and see her mother now. She was sure her mother wouldn't have called the police, but why else would the cops take him? They didn't search the place; Patrick hadn't been dealing drugs for quite a while.

Sonja hadn't been to see her mother since she'd moved in with Patrick. Maybe her mother really did want her to come back? She'd hoped, despite feeling like it was a bit of a betrayal to Patrick, that her mother would make an attempt to see her again. She hadn't expected the police though. This would make things ugly. Patrick had told her what the police were like to deal with. Nothing like Water Rats or Blue Heelers; but liars. Violent liars. And her parents had never trusted them. So why would her mother call them?

She'd have to go and sort this out.

She could smell her mother the instant she opened the door. She'd worked up so much shaky courage in the stairwell, and now this smell was melting her resolve.

—Hi, Mum, she said, looking directly at Katerina.

Her mother chewed the inside of her cheek, something Sonja had never seen her do before, and began to cry a little. Maybe it was anger.

—Sonja. Where is he? Katerina asked, looking past her daughter and down the stairwell.

—Where do you think? Sonja snapped, her anger partly due to her nervousness about seeing her mother again.

—What do you mean? Sonja, please don't come here to fight with me, not today.

—Did you call the police on Patri — me and Patrick?

—Don't say his name, Sonja. Don't say his name like that. Like he is your husband.

—Did you call the police?

—What do you mean, Sonja? No.

—Please. Don't lie to me, Mu —

—Do you want to see your father?

—Have you told him yet, Mum?

—He's home, Sonja.
—Oh.

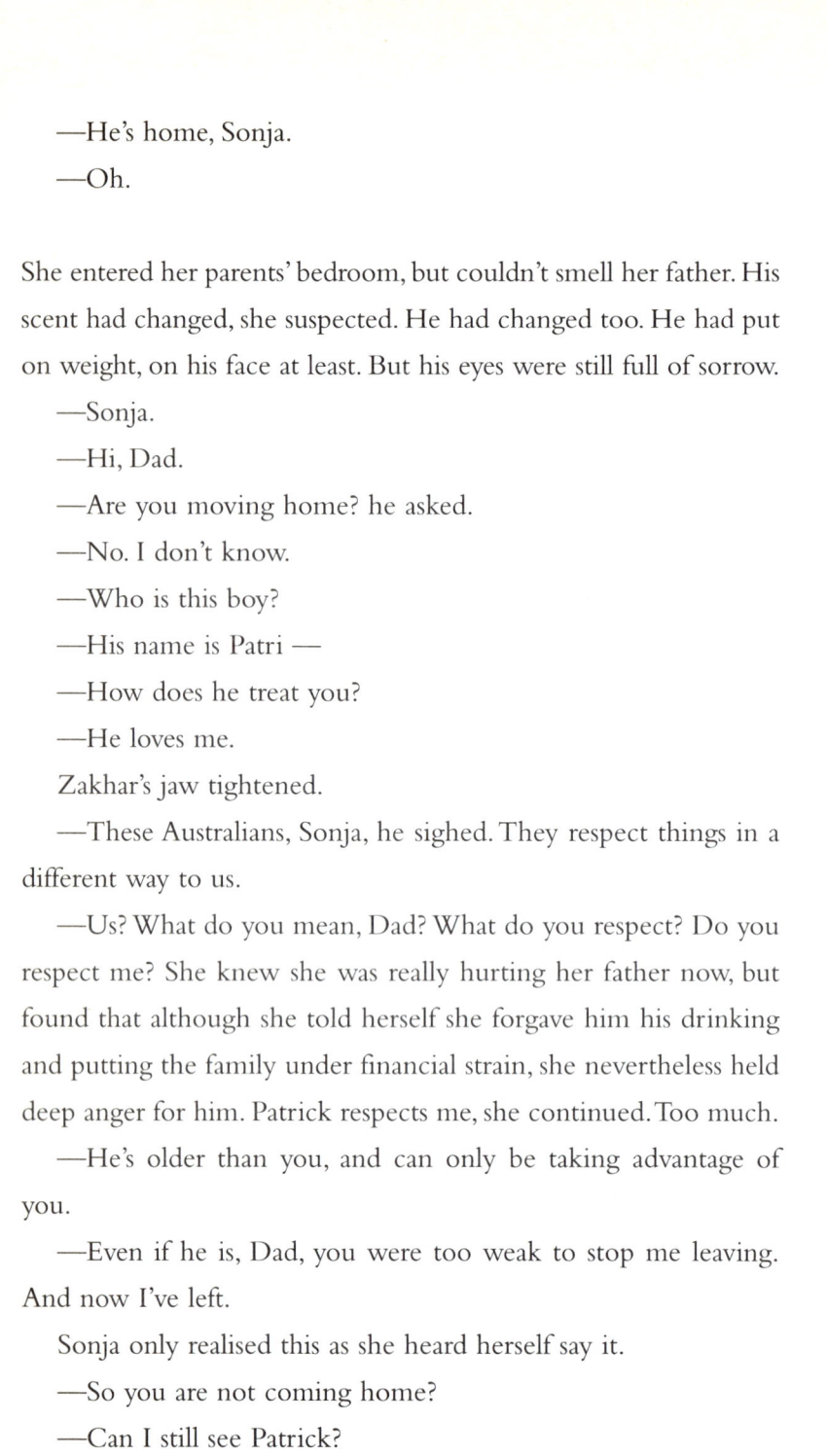

She entered her parents' bedroom, but couldn't smell her father. His scent had changed, she suspected. He had changed too. He had put on weight, on his face at least. But his eyes were still full of sorrow.
—Sonja.
—Hi, Dad.
—Are you moving home? he asked.
—No. I don't know.
—Who is this boy?
—His name is Patri —
—How does he treat you?
—He loves me.
Zakhar's jaw tightened.
—These Australians, Sonja, he sighed. They respect things in a different way to us.
—Us? What do you mean, Dad? What do you respect? Do you respect me? She knew she was really hurting her father now, but found that although she told herself she forgave him his drinking and putting the family under financial strain, she nevertheless held deep anger for him. Patrick respects me, she continued. Too much.
—He's older than you, and can only be taking advantage of you.
—Even if he is, Dad, you were too weak to stop me leaving. And now I've left.
Sonja only realised this as she heard herself say it.
—So you are not coming home?
—Can I still see Patrick?
—No.

—Then no. I don't want to — I don't want to come home right now.

But being back here, it suddenly struck her that maybe she did want to be back home. She had to leave her father, so he wouldn't read her thoughts. She went back into the kitchenette where her mother was standing with Peter, her brother.

—Peter, she said, and grabbed him. He hugged her back, tightly, and she did the same so he would feel she still loved him.

—I want to see my brother and sister. And I want to take some of my stuff.

—Take your clothes, Katerina said.

—I want some stuff for school, too.

—He lets you go to school?

—Of course. Why wouldn't he?

—Because he's making a wife out of you, a girl.

—He wants me to go to school. It's me. Sometimes I choose not to go. But I am still going to school, Mum.

It was best that she stay at school. For all concerned. She and Patrick had agreed. But it was hard, when he was at home all day. And the days at home with him were a whole world away from time and school. She should make more of an effort, though. She'd have to talk to Patrick tonight.

If he returned tonight.

She felt a bit weird about coming back to Patrick's flat. It was her home now too, but there was no comfort here. The comfort left with Patrick. Without him, she felt homeless. There wasn't enough of her here. It felt like Patrick had most of her with him, and his return would make her whole again. She needed to vomit, but hadn't eaten anything to facilitate it. She didn't know how she'd cope tonight if Patrick didn't come home. She didn't know if she could stop herself from going back to her parents' place so she could sleep with her sister. She couldn't sleep alone. Not tonight.

She looked out the window, into the courtyard of sun-killed grass husks, and to the ghost gum and the grey sky behind. It was a cold-looking day, but the humidity begged to differ. She turned on the television, but heard the concrete steps echo with footfalls outside the door and switched it off.

There were three firm knocks.

Sonja breathed as silently as she could and slowly moved to the door. Patrick had a piece of black cardboard over the peephole so visitor's couldn't see anything moving inside the flat. Patrick had told her there could be times when he had to avoid people. Sonja had assumed it was because of drugs. But maybe he could predict something like this happening. Because there was only one person Sonja would let in now. And as she lifted the cardboard and looked through the peephole, she saw that it wasn't Patrick.

The cops knocked again three times. Sonja nearly swore. She saw a cop's head move toward the peephole so she slid the cardboard back over it. She stepped away from the door. Her bladder burned. Adrenaline was hot in her arms. She had to look again. Three more knocks. She looked through the peephole. The cops were checking a black folder. One of them disappeared from view and she heard the neighbour's door pounded three times. Old Sid. She'd heard Patrick talk to him a couple of times. They'd met some of the same people in prison. She doubted if he'd answer the door to cops.

The cops left, slipping a worn NSW Police Force card under the door. Contact ASAP was written in red pen above a Constable Polkinghorn's name and number. Sonja threw it on the bench as she poured greyish tap water into the biggest glass Whitey had.

NINETEEN

The tattoo gun's buzz became more annoying than the pain caused by the needle. Abdullah was worried that the expression on his face when the needle first broke skin would betray him, but he could tell Fadi was jealous regardless. And he did truly get used to the pain about five minutes into the session. The Aussie biker had thrown him a look when Abdullah pulled out the Lebanese flag design. But he'd done the tatt anyway, without saying a word.

It was looking, and feeling, powerful. It was something to be proud of. Something people would remember of him.

—You gonna get one, mate? Abdullah asked Fadi.

The biker gave him that look again.

—Soon, mate. When I get the cash together, Fadi replied, and looked at the biker.

—Yeah fuckin' right, mate, Abdullah said, and the biker grabbed his arm hard to steady it.

Abdullah looked down at the biker's work. The green ink was staining inside the lines of the cedar tree. A thought as penetrating as the gun struck him. He'd never been to Lebanon. In fact, he'd never even really thought of going there. He was no fuckin' Aussie though. This country was full of dickheads, but he wasn't one of them, and this tatt would make that difference clear.

The biker bandaged the wound on Abdullah's shoulder.

—Don't pick at it. You'll tear the colour out if ya scratch the scabs off. Stay outa fuckin' trouble, hey boys.

—No worries, mate, Abdullah said, and extended his hand to the biker.

The biker scratched his stomach and went back into the tattooing room at the back of the shop.

Out on the main drag, Abdullah felt the energy of the pain in his shoulder. The Cross was alive with this sort of energy on any Friday night. Abdullah had fucked his first slut up here not too long ago. Ninety bucks, but fuck, it was mad. Better to get a free fuck though, he thought. The energy, like the wound it came from, was starting to become uncomfortable for Abdullah.

—See that Aussie biker cunt? Thinks he's too good ta shake my fuckin' hand. Lucky I didn't smack 'im one and take me two hundred bucks back.

—Yeah. Dickhead, Fadi said, and looked at the bandage on Abdullah's shoulder. Are ya gonna tell ya dad?

—Huh? Dunno. Fuck 'im.

Fadi could feel Abdullah's discomfort.

—So, what are we doin' tonight? Fadi asked.

—I'm gonna give Mia a call. You can hang if ya want. 'Cept when I'm givin' her one in the back of the car.

There were five or six Aussies having a piss-up at one of the barbecue tables in the park. They looked older than him — maybe thirty — but it was hard to tell with the Aussies: their flat faces and hard drinking showed age too early, Fadi thought. He was already in sight of them, and Abdullah would freak if he went back to the car now, so he kept walking towards them.

—Howsitgoin', mate? one of them said.

—Good, Fadi replied, and nodded at them.

—What's happenin'? the Aussie continued.

—Just havin' a session, mate, Fadi said. But my mate's busy with his missus.

—Fuckin' good on 'im. Wanna beer?

—Nah.

—Don't ya drink, mate?

—Nuh.

—Smoke but don't drink, hey. So what kinda wog are ya? the Aussie said and opened another beer.

—Leb, mate.

—Yeah, you Muslims don't touch the piss, do ya?

—Nuh.

—Ya should give it a try, mate. Mellow ya out.

—Thanks, mate, I'm mellow enough. So, does it give ya a good hit, mate, the beers?

—Fuckin' hit? The Aussie laughed. Fuckin' best hit.

Fadi doubted he'd like the hit of beer. He didn't even enjoy the hit of pot. But he'd started now, and to tell Abdullah and the others that he didn't want to smoke anymore would be more uncomfortable than that first twenty minutes of stoned paranoia after each session.

—Well, you guys have your hit, and we have ours, hey? he said.

—Mate, we have both, the Aussie laughed again. That's the good thing about this country. Ya can have piss, smoke, and whatever else ya fuckin' want as well. We're free here. Not like you poor bastards. Chained to ya religion and ya old ways 'n' that.

—I was born here, mate, like you, Fadi answered.

—You might have been born here, but not like me you weren't.

The whole group erupted in laughter. Fadi moved to look back at the car. He couldn't see either Abdullah's or Mia's head. He walked away from the Aussies regardless.

Abdullah had pulled it out this time at least. He said he hated condoms. She was nearly there too. If he had had a condom on, and just left it in for another minute, or even thirty seconds, she would have fully gotten there. He wiped himself with a small towel and put it on the puddle of come on her stomach. He did up his jeans and got out of the back of the car and back into the driver's seat.

—So what took ya so long tonight? We were waitin' at the bottom of ya street for forty fuckin' minutes, he said.

—My dad, she replied. He doesn't want me to go out. Some girls have been raped in the suburbs recently. I had to really convince him. It's getting harder to convince him too. We might have to cool it for a while.

—Fuck 'im. Raped? Ya can tell 'im I'm the only one rapin' ya, Abdullah laughed.

—Don't, Abdullah. It's serious. If he found out I was having sex with you, and if he found out you were Lebanese, he'd kill us both.

—What's wrong with Lebs? We're the best lovers. He should be happy you're gettin' the best.

—I'm serious. We're going to have to cool it for a bit.

—What about ya brother? Is he allowed out?

—What is it with you and my brother? Mia asked, raising an eyebrow in mock suspicion.

—Why, what's he told you?

—Nothing. But if Dad's getting stricter with me, he'll probably be stricter with him too, you know, so I won't be able to complain that he lets Charlie go out and not me.

—What about if I only ring you once a week for a while then? Ya gotta give us at least one root a week, Abdullah said.

—Please don't talk like that. It's meant to be a nice thing we're doing. You don't have to make it seem so — I don't know, crude. Maybe wait for a bit. I'll call you.

—What, so I can't even root my girlfriend when I feel like it now?

—Abdullah…

Abdullah finished his third set of thirty reps on the bench-press. Forty kilos. He got up and looked in the mould-stained mirror he'd propped up against the doorless wardrobe where his dad kept his tools. Gettin' cut up. More sit-ups are needed but, Abdullah thought. Sex is s'posed ta make ya fit. Need ta be bangin' more bitches. He flexed and scowled into the mirror, stretching the damaged and inked tissue of his shoulder. Fuckin' unbeatable, mate.

—Make sure you pack up these exercise things and put the car back in, Abdullah, his father said, walking past the side door of the garage and adjusting the nozzle of the garden hose.

—Yeah, Abdullah said, and then to himself: *Just water ya fuckin' wog trees. Dickhead.*

—And then come inside. I want to show you something, his dad added, reappearing in the doorway.

His dad sat at the kitchen table, still in his State Rail uniform. Abdullah came in wearing a long-sleeved T-shirt. Bet ya it's about the bandage on me arm, he thought.

—There's something in the paper I think you should look at.

—What are you talkin' about?

Abdullah's father slid the paper over to his son.

—I think you should think seriously about this.

Abdullah looked at the open page in front of him. It was the furthest thing from his mind. The employment section.

—There's a couple of jobs you could do, Abdullah.

—What are ya talkin' about? I've got a job. You got it for me, 'member?

—Abdullah, you may not be able to go back to the railways.

—What? Do you agree with those fuckin' Aussies?

—Don't swear at me. You should get another job anyway. It could be a while. Sam Spiropolous was on suspension for two years before they got rid of him for going to the internet things on the station computer. Perno, porno, or whatever you call it.

—Dumb Greek, Abdullah laughed.

—Then you should be smart and look for something else.

—All right. I'll look. Later.

Abdullah's father left the table. His usual gesture when he was frustrated with his son. When Abdullah heard the back door slam on to the plywood frame he looked down at the paper.

But Abdullah quickly bored of the employment pages. Why was it necessary to have all the shit they ask for: communication skills, customer service skills, experience in this thing and that fuckin' thing. Cunts should be happy if people just turned up to a place they didn't want to be. He flicked through the pages, looking at the women in the various images that had made it to print that day. Not much talent. He began to look at the words. Shit that mainly Aussies would be interested in. Cricket scores, golf stuff; shit about banks, and political cunts; Aussie troops in the Middle East (fuckin' cunts); rapes. Rapes.

Man Questioned in Connection with Teenage Rapes

Police from the Western Plateau Local Patrol questioned a 26-year-old man with prior drug convictions yesterday. It's alleged that as many as five, and possibly more, teenaged girls have been molested and raped in Sydney's west in the past six months. The man was not charged, but police say that he has helped them with their inquiries and that the perpetrators of these rapes will not get away with this kind of 'callous and cowardly behaviour' for any longer. Police warn parents of teenagers all over the city to ...

Abdullah scanned the article for names. There were none. Who was this cunt? A man. What fuckin' man? Rapes. One of those last chicks they fucked — the one who Fadi pulled the starter pistol on — she'd called them rapists. Rape? Abdullah shook his head, bewildered. Maybe, but a fuck's a fuck. But Fadi said later on that he didn't want to pick up chicks that way anymore. That it was a bit fucked-up to be going through all that to get a root. That he'd prefer to just get a girlfriend. And that he'd really scared that chick with the pistol — he'd felt a bit sorry for her.

Rape. Fuck. Isn't rape when you bash them and kill them? If this has come out of that last chick talking to the pigs, telling them she was raped, that's just fucked. She'd let them do it to her. The starter pistol was just a joke. And she'd agreed to a suck already anyway. All the chicks they'd picked up had let them. And they hadn't killed any of them. Hadn't bashed them either. Couple of slaps, but not beat them up. Shouldn't they like having so many blokes? I'd dig having five chicks root me, he concluded. They said they didn't want to do it, but all chicks say that, don't they? And they had agreed to come with us. They knew the deal. And anyway, like my uncle says, all these Aussies, all these non-Muslims, need sorting out. The country needs sorting out. Chicks walking the streets half-naked. Teenagers allowed to carry on with the opposite sex. Families go to the pub instead of church. All the laws favour the Christian Aussies. And we're meant to fit in with them, their fucked ways. Me and the boys are just stirring it up a bit. And having a bit of fun with the sluts. We're a gang, like the Crips and the Bloods in LA, but also like the Hezbollah. Offensive jihad, like my uncle talks about. We have to be hard cunts. We have to take what's not offered to us. Right?

Callous and cowardly?

Who knew about this? What cunt is talkin' to the cops?

What the fuck does callous mean?

The receptionist at the *Telegraph Post* couldn't, or wouldn't, help Abdullah with any names. She told him to ring the police, which he did — first making sure his own number-sending was switch off on his mobile. The only name they were interested in was his though. But he didn't give it. Not that fuckin' stupid.

TWENTY

Artemesia Testafiglia left school early. She couldn't focus on what anyone was on about: teachers or students. She'd been in some kind of agitated state since she last spent time with Abdullah. He'd always had some kind of effect on her, and when it was a new experience she'd loved it. But now it was getting to be a bit out of her control. This last intoxication was just unpleasant. And she couldn't shake it.

There were some boots at a mall out west that Mia had fallen in love with when she went shopping with Deba the week before. They were high, but had a slender foot — exactly what she'd been looking for to go with some lately purchased but unworn skirts. At two hundred and fifty dollars they'd shocked her mother, but she really had no idea. If she were to buy the same boots in her area — the north-west — she'd be paying at least three fifty. It's amazing what a difference a few suburbs can make. Mia had gotten hold of her mother's Visa card to buy a new jumper for school, but the jumper, of course, could wait.

Mia got on the westbound bus and flashed her student card. It was full of geriatrics, so she sat up the back, behind a westie couple.

The agitation resurfaced. She used to enjoy thinking about Abdullah between times when they were together, to be topped up by his smell, attitude and touch. But now she needed a dry stretch. Maybe. She didn't know what to do. He was hot. She'd invested a lot in him — deliberate betrayal of her parents, or her father at least; her body, her virginity; and so much mental energy. But lately, she'd been starting to miss her pre-Abdullah life — the sense of security her father had created for her. She'd wanted a relationship so badly before she met Abdullah, and he, a hot, confident guy, had made it possible. But maybe Daddy was right: she was too young to judge guys. Mia burped bile, because she hadn't eaten all day. She covered her mouth to stifle the impulse. It seemed to work.

She glanced over at the westie couple. They weren't paying attention to her, so she felt a little easier about her nausea. The guy had potential, but needed to cut his hair short and get some new clothes. Westies love that faded look, like they want to prove that Levis and T-shirts can outlast any fashion trend. The girl was young, or maybe just small. She too needed a hair consultant and, although she had on new and not inexpensive jeans, her shoes didn't go, and the shirt looked like it could be her boyfriend's. The guy touched the girl's hair and looked at her. He gazed into her eyes. He said one or two words, but his eyes were communicating most of what he wanted to say. They both laughed softly and then kissed. It was short, but Mia could tell it was enjoyable — she felt some of it and wanted to touch the guy's arm. It was a kiss of reassurance, of bonding, of something between only them. The guy put his arm around the girl and held her closer. The girl looked into his face and they kissed again. He seemed to respect her. Their physical closeness was so mutual. There was sexual attraction between them, but also so much love. Or at least something beyond just sex.

The couple also got off at the mall. Mia noticed the guy smelling the girl's hair as they stood waiting for the back doors of the bus to open. She wondered if the girl knew he did this. She wondered if Abdullah had sniffed her hair. She doubted it. She doubted that Abdullah had for her any of the feelings this guy held for his girlfriend. Abdullah liked to ejaculate freely and selfishly and drive away in his little car. There, she had admitted it to herself. Because Mia knew she had to start hating Abdullah in order to dispel him.

TWENTY-ONE

Patrick had been distant since his return from the police station. He'd held Sonja — as soon as he'd come in the door. But his expression had been too neutral. And he hadn't wanted to talk about the incident; just told her that it was all a fuck-up — a big mistake. He'd seemed pleased that she hadn't opened the door to the cops when they'd come back, three times all up, but his happiness appeared to evaporate as soon as he looked away from her. She'd cried, and Patrick had held her again. She didn't tell him she'd gone back to see her family. But she would tell him. When he seemed happier. When she was happier.

—I have ta get a job, he said after a couple of days of not really communicating much.

—Okay. Um, why? she asked, sensing from his tone that working was akin to putting a beloved pet to sleep.

—The dole's not enough for both of us. I can't sell, at least for a while, and I can't claim dole for you, I don't think, so, ya know, I guess I should get a job.

—Oh, Sonja replied. I'm sorry.

—Come here, you. He pulled Sonja close and hugged her. It'll be good. I think I want ta work.

—What will you do?

—Dunno. This West Work joint keeps sendin' me letters, tellin' me to come in and see them for an appraisal. Part of my dole conditions. I have to lie about looking for work on my form every fortnight anyway. I guess I'll go an' see 'em.

—Okay. As long as we stay together. And stay happy, Sonja said, and kissed Patrick's neck because he was finally including her in his thoughts again.

They caught the bus to the West Work office near Mt Druitt Mall. Sonja took the day off school. She wanted to be there with him to gauge this situation. It seemed like such a significant step forward. One she hadn't really even thought of, but one that now filled her with hope. And Patrick seemed to want her there. She waited in the foyer while Patrick watched OH&S videos and completed assessments. She read the dry literature on offer that boasted of people's happiness with West Work's services. But listened to the complaints people made to the receptionist about how they'd been sent to the wrong job; hadn't been paid; hadn't been paid; hadn't been paid; hadn't been sent to any jobs at all. She felt empty. She felt sorry for herself and for Patrick. The hope they seemed to share walking in here now felt futile.

Patrick emerged from the carpeted offices off the foyer. He flashed some paperwork at her and folded it into his back pocket.

—We're goin' by the Rooty Hill Plaza ta drop in an application. Greedos is lookin' for people. The chick already rang 'em. I might have a job within a week.

—Good. Are you happy? she asked.

—I guess.

They caught the bus from Mt Druitt to Rooty Hill. They were back in love. They were close and communicating. No one could ruin what they had. Though one thought did land heavily in Sonja's mind as they got off the bus at the plaza: she needed his happiness to be happy herself. Or the surprising happiness she felt when she'd visited her family. It was an isolating feeling. Why were her emotions so entwined with others'? And why did she feel she'd have to choose who she'd be entwined with?

The bottom of his bank account was starting to show. The Housing Commission, Electroturbine Company and Telecomonopoly dug out without notice — it was the only way they'd accept Whitey as a customer — and usually they were the only withdrawers. But without his cash income, Whitey had had to start using his dole payment. He'd been told that, as soon as the Greedos pay-office had processed him, he would be paid weekly. Three hundred and thirty a week after tax. More than the dole. But way less than the combination of selling and the dole. He'd also been told that he had to wear a white shirt and black pants. He didn't own any of the type they were talking about, so he'd had to make another withdrawal. Tomorrow he'd be a back dock assistant/shelf-replenisher. He walked past Greedos for the last time as a free man, with his white shirt and black pants in the C Mart bag. He met Sonja after school and showed her the contents of the shopping bag. She laughed.

—I can't wait to see you in them, she said.

The staff trainer bent over the bottom drawer of the dented filing cabinet. She had a pale blue g-string on, Whitey noticed. He looked at his boots as she turned around to face him.

—Read and sign this, Paul, she said.

—Okay. It's Patrick. My name's Patrick.

—What? Patrick, is it? Okay. Read and sign this. It's an outline of the company policies.

Greedos Pty Ltd

Greedos = Less Pty Ltd

Big G Pty Ltd

Dear <u>Mr</u> Miss Mrs Ms White

You have been made an offer of employment as a Back Dock Assistant/Shelf Replenisher. You will be employed on a probationary basis for a period of three months. Within this time you must demonstrate that you meet the requirements expected of Greedos employees, and adhere to Greedos company policies. After this period you will be assessed for future employment.

A summary of the policies are as follows:

- Greedos employees must promote Greedos, Greedos = Less, and Big G at all times.
- Greedos employees must be ready to begin their shift at least five minutes prior to commencement, and be prepared to complete the execution of all tasks regardless of the time of completion of their shift.
- Greedos employees must not keep money on their person while at work.
- Greedos employees must be neat, clean-shaven and conservatively attired at all time.
- Greedos employees must notify management of any theft, by employees or customers.

- Greedos employees must provide a doctor's certificate if sick leave is taken.
- Greedos employees must adapt to any roster changes initiated by management.
- Greedos employees must respect —

Whitey looked up at the staff trainer. She was drawing little squares and colouring them in on a tax declaration. He skipped to the bottom of the page and signed it. If he wanted the job there was no use reading the policies: too bad if they sucked.

—Okay, he said.

—Finished? Okay, let's go for a walk around the store.

The back dock was full of lamb carcasses. He shook the greasy hand of the apprentice butcher, and that of the back dock manager. The abattoir truck exhaled one last insult of diesel over the little skinned bodies as it left the dock. Whitey was then shown the cold storage area. It smelt like a nest of large wet dogs.

—It's the milk, the staff trainer explained.

Then the produce area. And the grocery area. And the vinyl flaps that led into the shop. Each part of the shop had a name that made no sense to Whitey, so he immediately forgot them. He looked at his watch — which he'd put on for the first time in about two years this morning — and wished it was knock-off time. It wasn't even time for morning tea. It reminded him of his first day inside. Being shown around and told how the joint operated. His chest hurt. He did have a choice though. He could fuck off now. No one would chase him. Nah, it'd get better. The pay 'n' all that. Once he was used to it. Just like inside. You can adapt to anything. He shook hands with and nodded at several people. The people were neutral at least. They knew why he was here. And didn't care much. Then he met Mr Hardy, Store Manager.

—Patrick, is it? Well, we're going to stick with the policies and keep the stock rotated, faced, and in constant stock aren't we, Patrick?

—Yes.

—Okay, well, welcome to Greedos Rooty Hill.

Mr Hardy didn't offer his hand so neither did Whitey. Whitey smiled though, and looked just past the manager. Mr Hardy wandered off to another stupidly named area of the store, rubbing his hands together. His slacks were pulled up way too high. But large, square arses did suit bosses.

Whitey was then given his first task. Emptying the meat, produce and general rubbish compactors. The compacted and plastic-sealed waste was then wheeled outside the loading dock area by pallet jack and left there for pickup.

—The last cunt left 'cause he had ta do that job every day, the back dock manager said, lighting a ciggie. Hasn't been done for a few days; ya must have a strong gut.

—I'm only just holdin' it down, Whitey replied.

—Well, after that ya can mop out the cold storage area. Now that's another top job, Pete.

—Patrick. Name's Patrick.

—Mmm.

TWENTY-TWO

Mia was starving. She'd been having these stupid waves of nausea followed by ravenousness. She knew why too. It was because of Abdullah. She had to talk to him, to tell him about how she was feeling. Because for her, it was over between them. She'd thought she'd loved Abdullah. And she thought she could forgive some of the things he'd done, the way he sometimes behaved. But really, how could she love someone who'd hit her? She'd forgiven him, she'd been fair; but whenever the thought crept back into her head, it made her ill. He'd done it. He'd hit her. That was the reality, and he could do it again. But he wouldn't. She wouldn't let it happen. And the way he talked to her sometimes. Worse than the way he spoke to his mates. She wanted to be serious with someone, and in love with someone, but she couldn't picture Abdullah as that someone any more. She had to tell him. Tell him it was over. But she knew that this was little more than a fantasy until she broke the news to him. And until she did she'd feel sick. But still, she couldn't finish dialling his number once she'd started. After dinner though, it'd have to be done.

—Mia, mangiare! her mother called.

At least someone's happy, Mia thought, now at the dinner table. Mum loves it when I eat; she barely eats herself, but makes sure everyone else makes pigs of themselves. She took another piece of chicken and flopped it on her plate. She couldn't remember the last time she'd had any more than half a piece of her mum's parmigiana.

—I think we'll have to have chicken seven nights a week, Maria, Salvatore remarked. We've finally found something our daughter will actually finish.

—Dad! Don't make me sound like a pig.

—It's good, Mia. You're too skinny. The last thing you have to worry about is getting fat, her father replied.

—You can never be too skinny or too rich, Dad.

—Don't be stupid, Mia. Too much of anything is — is unnatural.

—All right. Do you have to argue about everything I say, Dad?

—I'm not arguing with you, Mia, but some of your attitudes—

She'd had his number displayed on the screen of her mobile phone for ten minutes. She was about to press dial, but stopped again. She went into the options and turned her own number-sending off, just in case she lost her nerve after pressing dial. She brought Abdullah's number back up and called. *Fuck it. Just do it.*

—Yo, Abdullah's voice answered.

—Hi, Abdullah?

—Yeah. Who's this?

—It's Mia.

—Mia. Baby. Ya numba's comin' up as silent. What's up?

—I just want to talk to you.

—I can come by later. About ten if ya want.

—No. No, I just need to talk to you. The thing is — I think we shouldn't see each other for a while.

—Huh? What do ya mean?

—Maybe we should just cool it for a bit.

—You've said that before. What the fuck do ya mean?

—I dunno. Just not see each other for a while. Have a break.

—What the fuck for? Why are you being a bitch? What's ya fuckin' father said?

—It's not him, Abdullah, it's me. I just need a break—

—You fuckin' some other cunt?

—Abdullah, don't be like that. It's not about other guys—

—I'll be 'round in ten minutes. Be at the bottom of your street.

—Abdullah, no—

He'd ended the call. She tried his number again. It went straight to his message bank. Fuck.

Mia sat in her room deciding whether or not to give in to the nausea. She called out to her brother, and waited until he'd come in then shut the door.

—I've just broken up with Abdullah.

—Good. I mean, if that's what you want.

—It is.

—I don't think he's suited to you. Or you to him.

—I guess.

—He's not faithful to you, Mia.

—What?

—I think he — sees other girls.

—Arsehole.

Mia's phone rang.

—Mia. Where the fuck are ya? Abdullah barked.

—I'm not going to meet you.

—Bullshit. Get down here.

—No.

—Fuckin' bitch —

Mia ended the call.

The WRX pulled into the driveway and the high beams flooded the front windows. The driver sounded the horn.

Mia and Charlie looked out her bedroom window and watched their father approach the car. He leant into the car window and then shook his head. He then brought his mobile up to his ear as the WRX backed out.

It would be a long night of explaining and then re-explaining. Her father never accepted anything the first time when he was pissed off.

Something shattered one of the double-glazed windows of the formal lounge as Salvatore Testafiglia climbed the stairs to his daughter's room.

He couldn't go home. His dad would piss him off. *Just lookin'* at him. He didn't want to see any of his mates. They wouldn't know how to act. He'd chucked that piece of garden tap through the bitch's window. Her dad's a fuckin' cop, too. She better explain to him that it's her fault for trying to dump him. He dropped the clutch through the intersection and saw the cop car, its strobing red and blue lights triggering his heart to beat in hot, involuntary unison. He pulled on the handbrake and punched the sun visor.

The ink wouldn't wash off. The cop wore rubber gloves when he took the fingerprints. At first Abdullah assumed the cop put the gloves on because the stupid skip didn't want to touch him. But the cop knew the black shit wouldn't come off. Then he had to have his photo taken. And a photo of his tatt. He flexed when the cop took that one. And the charge — Malicious Damage. That bitch's father is lucky I didn't damage her and him. Did damage her though. And she loved it. She'll be feelin' that fuckin' sorry now that her father'll be down here droppin' the charges very soon.

—Senior Sergeant wants to talk to you himself. He'll be here shortly, the cop said. You're either one very unlucky bastard, or one very stupid bastard.

—That guy says he's your boyfriend, Mia. Your boyfriend.

—He — he was.

—What the hell do you mean, was? You were sneaking around with that?

—I don't know — yes, I s'pose.

—Jesus, Mia. What did we decide about you having a boyfriend? Do you remember?

—You decided.

—That's right. I decided that my daughter can go out with a boyfriend when she's finished school. And your mother and I should meet him.

—You wouldn't like any boy I brought home.

—Can you see why? Jesus, girl, that guy, your boyfriend is — what is he? An Arab? An Arab and a bloody criminal. Have you seen the window? An Arab, Mia. An Italian boy, at least. I would have thought you had some taste.

—Daddy. I'm sorry. She began to cry.

—Mia. I don't know. I don't know what to think. You lied to us. And not just a little lie. And look what's happened.

Salvatore moved closer to his daughter.

—I'm sorry, she said, checking her eyes in the mirror. I swear, Daddy, I'm sorry.

—Mia. You won't see this guy again, will you? I'm serious, Mia. This ends here and now.

—I promise, Daddy, I was trying to break up with him. That's why he did this.

—I thought as much. Mia, I know boys are asking you out. But you have to say no. Look what's happened. You're beautiful, and boys will fall in love. But you don't want this, do you?

—No, Daddy.

—There'll be no more going out on your own, Mia. Not for a long time.

Mia hugged her father. Just a few weeks ago she couldn't even look at him. Now she didn't want him to leave. Because she knew if he left, when he came back he'd have that look again. It was pure hurt. She'd hurt him so much. Just a few weeks ago she wouldn't have cared if her father had gotten upset. He would have deserved it — for limiting her freedom. But now he was the answer. The situation with Abdullah was difficult but she knew Daddy would fix it now. She'd never have to see Abdullah again. She could feel completely sure that it was over. And she could live with whatever punishment her father had for her. And she could begin to win back his devotion.

Her father released his hug as his mobile rang. He grunted and ended the call.

—This boy won't bother us anymore. He's down at the station. I'll have a talk with him.

The boy was not even good-looking. Those dark, lying eyes. Skinny little Lebanese. He must be a good liar to have convinced Mia to go out with him. It hurt. Lurking in the back of his mind was the possibility that Mia might have slept with this thing.

He couldn't ask her. He'd rather not know, now that he was faced with it.

—You've got a court date next week. I'll see you there. But between then and now, and every day after that I don't want to see you. And my daughter will never see you.

—She wanted to see —

—You're lucky I'm a cop, mate. You've got a chance to put this behind you and never think of my daughter again. But if you choose not to put it behind you, I know some people who aren't cops who would love to have a word with you.

—What the fuck does that mean? Abdullah retorted, rubbing his shaved head.

—I have to leave now or I'll rip your fucking face off, Senior Sergeant Testafiglia said as he waved a threatening hand just centimetres from Abdullah Najib's nose.

He left the interview room. The blood vessels in his neck, pounding like a mudslide, were bringing him to the verge of vomiting.

TWENTY-THREE

Fadi tilted the load and felt the back end of the forklift jump from the weight. You should never lift two pallets stacked on top of each other, but fuck it. He cleared the pallets from the side of the trailer and transferred them into the receiving dock. It was his fifth semi-trailer this morning, and he'd had enough. The other two forkies — fuckin' Aussies — were the biggest fuckin' bludgers. Even Dicko, the foreman, admitted it. Aussies'll do anything to get out of work. That's why they'll always be losers. But are they losers? Is simply being Lebanese the key to being better, smarter, tougher than everyone else? He'd never thought about it. Why would he? Everyone he hung out with thought the same. Lebs are unbeatable.

But something deep inside him had been damaged — was slowly bleeding, he felt — since that last girl they'd been with. With the other girls they'd done it to, there'd been a kind of shared energy that had erased any misgivings about what they were doing. They were doing it, the Punchbowl Leb boys, so it was right, it was tough, it was showing these Aussies that the Leb boys could do what they wanted to, it was getting laid — fuck, it was even funny. But that last one, she'd shown him something. Or maybe exposed something in him that had become vulnerable for that moment when he was on top of her. He couldn't work out exactly what it was, but since then his whole life — the way he'd been living it — seemed askew.

In fact, he'd not been able to get her out of his mind. She'd freaked when he'd pulled the starter pistol on her. He'd thought that her fear would turn him on, but instead, it seemed to transfer to him. He'd tried to mechanically go through with it — 'cause the boys were there — but he'd felt sick, was about to spew, and had had to get away from her before the fear she was giving to him overwhelmed him. Then Ali had jumped straight on her. When he thought about it now it filled his veins and his neck muscles with icy hot acid.

But there was another feeling. One that was more intimate. One that was a comfort and quite opposite to the other one. She was so pretty. He kept thinking of her. Not in the situation they'd put her in, but natural, with her prettiness unchanged by that expression of terror. He'd actually almost seen her like that, in the flesh, when he'd first gotten in the car with her. Sure, she'd looked pissed off, and maybe a little scared, but still bright and alive. That fuckin' pistol had wiped that vitality from her. And he wished so much that he could have that moment back, and not have brought out that stupid gun, and become her rescuer. He'd nearly cried a couple of times when he'd thought about it. Fuckin' rapists, she'd said. Yelled it, crying.

He'd driven her and her friend back to the mall afterwards and he'd looked at her every chance he got, at red lights and that. She was beautiful — like a child with sticky tears on her slightly chubby cheeks. Abdullah had taken her mobile, and Fadi had asked for it. He had it at home. He kept it on and checked it constantly just in case she called it. No one had called it. He really wanted to see her again. He couldn't bear the fact that she must hate him. He wanted to at least apologise. He tried not to think about her, but he noticed something of her in nearly every chick he saw. And there must be a chance that she didn't hate him, mustn't there? *Just like her fear had rubbed off on him, mustn't what he'd been feeling have made an impression on her?*

After morning tea he was going to go home sick. Fuck those two Aussie dickheads; they can handle the rest of the day.

His mum was hassling him. He hadn't been eating much lately and she was convinced that it was the reason he'd come home sick.

—I'll make you some eggs, she said. The third time now.

—No, Ma. I'm orright. Done worry about it.

—I'll make you some. You probably caught something off those swine-eaters you work with.

—Ma.

He shut his bedroom door and sat on his bed. He picked up her phone. He'd tried to ban himself from thinking about her. He'd started to love her name. And it filled him with a hot, thick, sick feeling that he couldn't identify whenever it snuck into his head. He didn't even know her name when he'd — been on top of her; Abdullah had told him later. Tennille. But maybe it was okay. It didn't feel as bad as usual. Because he was going to talk to her. He had to.

He'd scrolled through the phone's address book a hundred times. There were some names in there that fuckin' cut him. Brad, Davo, John, Mick, Scott. Aussies. All Aussie guys. She could be fucking one of them. All of them. He hated that she knew so many guys. But there was also a number that held promise. Work. It must be her work.

He brought it up and pressed dial.

—This service has been cancelled. Please call Telecomonopoly inquiries on 13 13 —

Of course, he sighed. She would've cancelled her phone. He brought up the details of Work to get the number.

—Ma. Bring the phone will ya!

His mother brought him the phone and told him not to be long. She said the same thing every time anyone used the phone. He doubted she even knew what it meant anymore.

He dialled the number.

—Hollywest Cinemas, the voice said.

Fadi waited in case it was a recorded message.

—Hi. Is Tennille there?

—Can you tell me what section she works in, please?

—Ah — nuh.

—Okay. Tennille is it? Tennille who, sir?

—I dunno her last name.

—Please hold.

He waited and scratched his back. He was doing it. He was ringing her.

—Hello.

—Hi, he said. He wasn't sure if it was the same chick he'd just been talking to.

—Who's this?

—Who's this? he said.

—Tennille. Who's this?

—It's Fadi.

—Fadi? Fadi who?

—We — we met a few weeks ago.

—When? Where?

—I came to the park. You were at the park with my mates. Remember?

—Who is this?

—Fadi.

—How did you get my work number?

—I've got your phone.

—You what? You've got my phone. You arsehole. I — I want it back.

—Okay — okay. I want to give it back.

—Take it to the police station.

—I'll bring it to you.

—No. Take it to the police station.

—You work at Hollywest?

She was silent but he could hear noises in the background.

—I'll bring it to your work, he repeated.

—*Jesus*! Take it to the police. Don't come here.

—I'll be there soon. I'll just give it to you. I want you to have it back.

Fadi's mother came in with the eggs.

Tennille had gone pale, but her cheeks began to colour with stress-borne hives. This fucker had the gall to ring her. She looked over at the tense-barriers that they used to herd patrons into the cinemas. Could she use one of the posts to wrap around his head if it came to it? *Jesus.* He was about to turn up here. She couldn't face him. This was just too unfair. Why does it just keep getting worse? Why can't this shit end?

Tennille had gone back to work, gone back to uni after two weeks. No one except Melissa, who'd flown to London with her mother a week after the rape, and Greer, one of her workmates —

who seemed to sense that something heavy had happened to her, so she'd told her — knew about what she'd been through. So she could try and get on with her life, her parents had said. Get on with it? How the hell do you get on with it? Everything is changed. Getting on with it meant dragging it everywhere she went, and through everything she did. What those animals had done to her coloured every aspect of her life now. There were moments when it would slip out of her mind, and she felt like a carefree, happy young woman, but then it would flood back in, and for a moment feel like it was something outside her existence, but then the feeling of dread would quickly set in, and be back, filling her up. The knowledge that she was sharing the world with people — no, things — that had violated her in that way.

The counsellor had told her it was up to her how much she wanted to talk about it. It was up to her to go forward with the charges if they caught these pricks. Up to her if she wanted to go back to work and school. But she didn't trust her own decisions. They'd caused her to get raped. And got her best friend raped. She'd decided to go with those arseholes, not Melissa; those arseholes who had made her take them in her mouth, and then pulled out a gun and made her lie down and have two of them thrust and grunt and groan and hurt her and put their stink all over her. The pig with the gun hadn't managed to enter her, but he'd pushed and pinned her down with his whole weight and then suddenly got off her. The other fucker had gotten himself inside her though. She'd turned into a corpse when the pain translated into what was actually happening. Her fear had actually allowed her to mentally escape what she was experiencing — it had sent her mind into a confusing collision of thoughts; until that disgusting thing had broken into her. She felt all her organs freeze, like they were giving up. And her body went into atrophy. She hadn't really been revived yet. She had no idea how long that second one was on top of her and inside her. She could still feel him now. The sensation would come and smack her. Like that first fucker's hand against her neck, but with a far deeper pain. But, like a zombie, she'd gone back to work and uni. It would help her get her life back, she was told. It seemed logical. But she didn't think the plan was working. She was strong — people had always said so. But how strong do you have to be?

—Jesus, Tennille. What's up? You don't look so hot, Greer said.

—One of those ... Tennille looked at her feet. One of those guys is coming here.

—What guys? Greer asked, and then: Oh.

—The ones I told you about. The ones who raped Melissa and me.

—What? Here?

—He's bringing my phone.

—Call the cops.

—Yeah. I'll wait to see if he turns up first. It could be someone being a dickhead, fucking with me.

—No one would be so cruel, surely. I'm going to call them.

—Will you get the phone off him? If he comes?

—You bet I'll get your phone off him. And I'll give him a kick in the nuts.

—Don't. Don't — You know, provoke him. *Just* in case.

—I won't. I'm sorry. It's just — I can't believe he'd fucking call you, Tennille. What is he thinking? That he'll have another go? Look, if he comes, I'll go down and keep him here until the police come. What do you think?

★

Tennille and Greer waited up on the mezzanine level where they could see the approach of everyone entering the cinema complex. Every guy with black, cropped hair panicked her. Tennille was praying that the police would arrive, but each minute seemed to eat away at her hope that they would even show up. Then she began to realise that she couldn't remember what any of the guys looked like. Not really. She could recall their smell. And that awful, awful feeling of their fingers. And their cocks — like sick, alien reptiles. But the visual had been mostly erased. Almost immediately. She'd looked at the rego of the car when she'd got out at the mall, but couldn't remember one number or letter when she'd had to repeat it to the cops.

But then she saw those eyes, darting around the foyer of the cinemas, and remembered them. It was the one. The cunt with the gun. She nearly ran. Out the fire exit. But continued to stare. He looked small. Like a boy. A kid. Nervous. The fucker.

—That's him, she said to Greer, and pointed at him. It.

—God, Greer said with a shudder.

He didn't look like a monster. He looked like a try-hard. A boy who thought he was a man. A follower. The exact same haircut as all his friends, Greer suspected. And a fucking idiot. The cops hadn't arrived yet. She'd have to talk with this creature.

—Have you got Tennille's phone?

—Huh?

—Have you got Tenni —

—Who are you?

—Her friend.

—Where's she? I wanna talk to her.

—Well, she definitely doesn't want to talk to you. What do you think you're doing turning up here and asking for her?

—Hey, I'm just tryin' ta be nice, he whined, and put his hand in his pocket.

—Have you got her phone?

—I'll only give it to her.

—I'll give it to her.

—I wanna see her. I wanna apologise.

Greer looked at this boy. He thought he could make it better. He thought he was doing something good here. He thought there was a possibility of redemption. With a phone.

—If you give the phone to me, it'll make her happy. I'll make sure she gets it. And anything you want to tell her, I'll tell her.

—Will ya get her ta call me?

—If she wants to.

The boy produced the phone. He looked at it. Greer could tell his plan, whatever it was, was disintegrating. He did still have the phone, though.

—I'll tell her you're sorry. And ask her to call you, she said.

He handed over the phone.

—I just wanna tell her that — he said, and looked over Greer's shoulder.

She thought, and felt her head nearly turn, that he'd spotted Tennille.

He turned and walked quickly to the escalators, and ran up them towards the street exit. Greer then saw the royal-blue-and-white chequered band on the cops' hats that had given away their approach.

TWENTY-FOUR

It was his first warning. You got three, before instant dismissal, he'd been informed. And even one could damage your chances of keeping your job if it came within your three months of probation. In a way it was worse than getting busted by the cops. At least with the cops he knew that he was doing something wrong. He was well aware that selling drugs was illegal. But here, in Greedos World of Grocery Bargains, he didn't know what the fuck he'd done. He was just informed by the assistant manager that, due to misconduct, he was to receive counselling.

—I have to see a counsellor? Whitey'd asked.

—No. You have to get a formal caution.

Whitey knocked on Tom Hardy's office door.

—Patrick. Come in. Close the door.

Whitey walked into the small makeshift office and shut the door. He stood still and felt very stupid.

—Patrick. Okay, mate. You've read the Shelf Replenisher's Handbook haven't you?

—The what? No — I don't think so.

—No? And why not?

—I don't know what that book is, Whitey replied, and looked at Tom Hardy for the first time since he'd come into the office.

—Well, all shelf replenishers must read it. It's your bible here.

—I don't have one. I wasn't given one.

—Well, you should have asked for one, Tom Hardy said, and picked up his pen — his fifteen years' service pen — and clicked three times.

—But I've never heard of this book, Whitey protested, and shifted; suddenly he needed to piss.

—Well, that's a problem. But it isn't mine, is it? My problem is that you've failed in your duties.

—Oh.

—Yes, oh. When we're filling the bottom shelves, do we sit slouched on the bottom of a stepladder, or do we squat neatly close to the shelf? Mr Hardy asked.

—Um, dunno.

—Dunno! Dunno! No, you don't know. Because you don't know your job, do you? You need to read your handbook.

—Okay. Sorry — so where do I get one?

—Look, Patrick, I'm giving you a second chance, don't get smart. You'll soon see the wrong side of me.

—Okay, Patrick said, and wondered if he should go now.

—So, Tom Hardy said, and clicked the pen again. Have you got a partner at home?

—Partner? A girlfriend you mean?

—Or boyfriend.

—Yeah, I've got a girlfriend, Whitey answered, and really wanted to go now.

He liked to keep any thoughts of Sonja completely to himself. His feelings about her were so personal — they got him through the day here — it felt wrong to discuss her with this guy.

—Girlfriend, hey? I thought you might be from the same side of the fence as myself, Tom Hardy said, and winked. No matter, he continued. You can get back to the cake-mix aisle now.

Jesus, Whitey mused as he opened a third box of Carboboosta cake mix. He thought I might be gay. He's gay. The manager's gay. I don't think I've ever been taken for gay before. Then his memory brought to the fore an old chestnut from not too long ago. Some of his sexual exploits while inside. *Jesus. Maybe I'm giving off that vibe now. Maybe what I did inside shows on the outside — to those who know what to look for.*

Whitey didn't have anything against gays. Didn't really know any. But he didn't want to be known as one. Or thought of as one. He wasn't one, was he? He'd done stuff with a guy. But he'd felt like shit afterwards. He thought about what he liked. Nah. He was more — if he was to be totally honest — tending towards being a paedophile. A heterosexual paedophile. *Jesus.* But, nuh. Before Sonja, he hadn't really thought about girls that much younger than himself. School uniforms never really did it for him before Sonja's. *Jesus.* He was gettin' too — what do ya call it? — self-analytical since he'd taken this job. Too much time to think about shit, without the distraction of drugs and sex with a teenager. *Jesus, shut up.*

—Patrick White to the back dock, grocery bulk-truck delivery, announced the PA speakers in the ceiling.

Thank fuck, Whitey sighed with relief. A distraction, of sorts. *Although there's most likely a handbook on truck unloading that I'm unaware of.*

★

He clocked himself off at the pay-office window at the end of his shift and, for the first time that week, headed straight for home. The deal here, at Greedos, was that if they still wanted you to do something right on knock-off time, you had to clock-off, and then come back and do the job. Overtime had to be pre-approved, but it never was, so the work was done pro bono, apparently.

He didn't mind the work. It was just all the rules. Even he, who'd had sparse experience in retail — in the workforce in general — could see that if he was able to do things his own way, he could get the job done just as well, if not better. Like filling the bottom shelves. By sitting on the bottom step of the stepladder with the boxes in front of him he could fill three times as fast as crouching down and having to twist the fuck out of his back to get the stuff from the box to the shelf. And if he was allowed to piss when he needed to instead of only on smoko breaks, he'd be able to keep his mind focused on the job instead of having to concentrate on ignoring the pressure pushing back up into his kidneys. Apparently he was lucky not to get a warning for pissing outside of break times.

He climbed the three steps to his flat and began looking for his keys. He had to get into a routine. One day he'd find his keys in his backpack, the next in his pants pocket, and on the third day they'd be in his jacket pocket. Today they were nowhere. It was only a matter of time. Sonja opened the door.

—You're home, he said.

—Yes, baby. How are you?

—Had a Barry Crocker.

—A — what?

—Shocker. A shocking day today.

—Why? What happened? Sonja asked, grabbing his hand and pulling him gently through the door.

—Nothin'. Don't worry.

—Oh.

—So, no library today? Whitey asked.

—No. Listen, Patrick. I've been going to see my family after school.

—Oh, he said. How are they?

—They're okay. Are you okay, I mean, with me seeing them?

—They're your family. Of course I'm okay with it. I'm just not sure why you thought I'd mind.

—So are you upset? A bit? she asked, and sat down.

—No. I mean — I'm upset about other shit. But no, not that. If you want to see them, like I said, they're your family. One thing though, Whitey said, and looked in the fridge.

—What, baby?

—What do they say about us? About me?

—They — they're a little concerned. But maybe a little less each time I've seen them.

—Oh.

—Can my brother and sister come here to visit? she asked.

—Yeah, of course they can. It's your place too, Sonja.

Whitey opened the last beer and took a long slug. He looked at Sonja. She was so cute. Innocent, yet intelligent. She had a lot of energy too, but could focus it. She would clean, read, do homework, and make love. She made him feel pretty slothish. She noticed him looking at her, and smiled. He smiled back, and drained off the beer. She glanced up at him again. He was still looking at her but not smiling.

—What's wrong, Patrick?

—Do we really love each other? he asked, and put the beer can down.

—What? What do you mean? Of course we love each other. I love you, Patrick. I definitely love you.

—Maybe we're just obsessed. You know, the sex and everything.

—Patrick. What do you mean? I thought it was good. No. I thought it was great. I love you. Don't you love me?

—I don't know. Yes, I love you but — you're young. I don't know. Don't you ever think I'm sick? I was thinking about it today. You know. Us being together. Me, living — having sex with — a schoolgirl.

—Oh.

—I mean — look, I'm sorry. I just had a shit day. I'm sorry, Patrick sighed, and held Sonja.

They didn't make love that night. The first time since she'd moved in. Patrick woke sometime before dawn and moulded himself into the contours of Sonja's body. It would be hard if they split up. The hardest thing he'd ever done, really. Because he realised that he'd never been paranoid about a girl. The dynamics of his relationships had never really bothered him one way or the other. But this one made him think. He did love Sonja. Why else would he feel this way? And despite all his questioning of the relationship, he didn't want to be without her.

Whitey got ready for work, pulled two cones, and brushed his teeth. It was the first time he'd smoked before work, but it seemed like a perfect time to start. Although, if he was going to make it a habit, he'd have to get some more heads — the bottom of the bowl was definitely showing. He'd kept some for himself when he'd moved the rest of his saleable stash to Ronnie's place. Lately he'd been indulging at night, after Sonja had fallen asleep.

He clocked on and went to make a coffee. Seven dollars a week was deducted from his wage to use the generic brand tea and coffee in the staffroom, so it was stupid not to indulge, even if it tasted like shit. For once he wanted to start work straightaway. Being stoned was making him keen. He went down into the back dock and pulled out a pallet from the immediate-fill bay and wheeled it into the shop. It was a different world here today. Being stoned made it something new. And it was always much better in the mornings before the shop opened to the public, and all the managers got in. He positioned the pallet in the feminine hygiene aisle and ripped off the shrink-wrap. He noticed the shop's lighting for the first time. It was harsh, but the products were all easy to see. He noticed that you could hear the staff — still relatively happy before their day of serving — joking and talking loudly. And he became aware that he'd been just standing in the aisle, not doing any work.

Whitey put the maternity pads to the front of the shelf and began on the mini tampons. He got halfway through the box and had to stop. He was thinking of Sonja. He'd planted a thought in her last night. It just hit him. Letting her know that he had doubts would make her doubt. He was sure of it. They'd become so close that their moods had begun to mimic each other. Patrick White nearly panicked. He nearly dropped the pack of tampons and walked out of the shop. He didn't want to split up with her. But he didn't want to get much closer either. He'd never been with a girl this long — not living together, that was for sure. And if it was already starting to freak him out, maybe it would become something he couldn't deal with. She'd be getting pressure from her parents too. Maybe he'd get home this afternoon and she'd be gone. His heart pumped strong waves of blood through his neck. He ran out into the back dock, pulled out his mobile and dialled her number. It rang. And rang. And got diverted to her message bank, which wasn't set up. Shit.

Such good pressure. One of the things she could remember about Russia was that the plumbing had no pressure. But here, even in public housing, you could get good pressure. And hot, hot water. She loved a long shower. It was hard to have one while living with her mother and father, as her mother would bang on the bathroom door after a couple of minutes — the electricity bill, she'd say. But since living with Patrick it was bliss. He was quick in the shower. Didn't seem to care for using it until the water ran out. She loved it. Loved that he let her do it. She loved to have the flat to herself too. She'd put the radio on, on Patrick's stereo. He liked that heavy metal stuff. She didn't mind it. Most of it was good. Very emotional. But you couldn't really dance to it. Sonja turned off the water: it was changing from lukewarm to cold. She got out of the recess and thought she heard her mobile phone. She froze, concentrated on everything beyond earshot of the leaking shower-rose. So many things sound like a mobile ring when you only hear a sliver of sound. No mobile ring.

She dried herself and regarded herself in the mirror. She had no idea what Patrick saw in her. But he seemed to like the way she looked, no matter what. But, *Jesus*. Maybe not. He doubts something about me. But there's no ambivalence in his touch. In the way he feels. The way he presses against me. Every night we're part of each other.

But not last night.

This was something she had to think about. The pill. She'd had two months' worth when she'd moved in with Patrick, but there were only two pills left. The doctor had prescribed it to help with her period pain. Killer pain.

She left the flat and went to pick up her sister. Her father was on the outside steps smoking a rolled cigarette.

—Hi, Dad, she said. How are you feeling today?

—Sonja. I am good today. I am going to the hospital this afternoon.

Her father was still an outpatient. And quite a dutiful one, it seemed. He'd found something in Australia to respect, her mother had told her. The healthcare professionals here were true public servants, her mother agreed.

—That's good, Dad. Polly and me will come to the hospital with you after school if you like. Is she ready?

—Go inside and see. This is still your home, Sonja.

She went in, unsure of whether her father expected a response. Polly was eating a triangle of barely browned toast.

—Ready, Poll?

Polly rolled her eyes. She liked school, Sonja thought, but was getting to the age when the world outside school begins to reveal itself as an infinitely more interesting place. Even a day off at home could be a secretly novel experience.

—Well, we're running late, Poll, let's go.

Her little sister stuffed the toast into her mouth and slung her schoolbag over one shoulder. Walking to school together was something Sonja had missed when she'd first moved in with Patrick. It was probably the main thing that had kept her going to school now. It made it more comfortable. Going straight to school from her lover's bed felt strange, awkward. Walking with Polly was a buffer between woman and schoolgirl.

—Bye, Dad, she said.

—Have you thought about it seriously, Sonja? her father asked.

—What do you mean? she replied, but knew.

—Coming home.

—Dad. Yes, I've thought about it. I'm still thinking about it.

—Seriously?

—Dad, I've got to go to school.

Sonja felt the side pocket of her schoolbag. It was something she did whenever she thought of Patrick. Because that was where she kept her mobile phone. She'd left it back at the flat. Shit. She didn't have time to go back for it. Patrick rarely rang since he'd started the job anyway.

They walked hand in hand through the streets that wound up towards their respective schools, Polly swinging their arms to a rhythm that Sonja easily adapted to. Her flat, her parents' flat, had felt different this morning. It had felt like a home. A family home. There was no tension. When she'd moved to Patrick's she had wanted to get out of there so badly. And she'd thought she'd never want to go back. Her mother was just a stress-head and impossible to live with when her father was drinking, and then in hospital. But things had changed since she'd been gone. They seemed calm. It was the way a family home should be. And she missed her brother and sister so much. She missed being their big sister. Sure, she was still their big sister now, but maybe too big a sister — living out of home with a boyfriend. She wanted to be there for them. And when she compared her two homes, one had gotten better, while the other — the one she was living in — had not really developed any further. And in fact, had just gotten a bit tense.

These thoughts had been fighting to come to the surface for a while now, she realised, and it seemed they'd broken through.

As Sonja walked through the school gates, she could sense someone looking at her. She looked sideways, quickly, to try and avoid any direct eye contact. But failed. The boy waved at her. It was Brett, Raz's friend. She waved back, and half-smiled. She'd thought she'd seen him waving at her once before, but had decided that he must have been directing the gesture at someone else; or just being a smart arse.

—Hi, Sonja, he said.

—Hi.

—How are you today? he continued, now walking beside her.

—I'm not too bad.

—You look good.

—Thank you, Brett.

TWENTY-FIVE

Charlie Testafiglia hated girls. He hated looking at them. And couldn't talk to them at all anymore. Even Sophia in his English class, whom he hadn't been able to stop looking at, thinking about, wondering about a month or so ago, now disgusted him. She was a completely different being now. Girls had flaws. He'd never imagined they would. Not the type he'd discovered anyway. Even his sister, who had turned into something perfect at age twelve, was a totally flawed being. She let someone like Abdullah — like him — do things to her. That girl, in the back of Abdullah's car, had made him come. She hadn't wanted to do it. He could tell by her expression. But her face had made him come. She knew what to do. He didn't even mean to come. He wished he hadn't. He hated that he had. And girls, all girls, reminded him of his weakness, his vulnerability.

The hatred had dawned gradually. In fact, it felt like it was still building. It wasn't a violent hate though. It just made him want to avoid females altogether. He was going to avoid Abdullah too. There was no way he was going to do that again. Abdullah had called Charlie though. There were probably fifty unanswered calls from him on Charlie's mobile. He wouldn't be able to avoid him for much longer. But he couldn't tell his dad — the one thing that would stop Abdullah — because it would kill him. Mia had already nearly killed him. The whole thing made him sick, and he hated it. And everything that was associated with it.

He was sweating, and didn't know what was going on in his class. People were moving, getting up, but it wasn't the end of the period. It'd only just begun.

—Charlie, Mrs Standish said, have you got a partner?

—No, I —

—Well, you pair up with Sophia, seeing as she's decided to finish her conversation with Theresa and Vicky rather than find a partner.

—Jeez, Miss, Sophia moaned.

—It's Mrs, Miss, Mrs Standish said. Now you two go out into the study room so Sophia won't be tempted to start another conversation.

—I'll be all right by myself, Charlie said, but Mrs Standish had turned away and was organising another pair.

Sophia left the classroom without looking at Charlie.

—Come on, Charles, she said in a mock posh tone.

He would have found it so sexy a couple of months ago, but now he felt all the blood drain from his body and into his stomach. He got up on shaky legs.

The study room was exceedingly hot. The air was thick, and moving it through his chest was like inhaling jelly. Sophia was talking, but the words sounded like the front gate at home that clanged through the side passage when it slammed. He hated that sound. It was so hot. The air was turning into heat. His neck muscles went slack. He thought he was going to vomit the hotness. Then his leg muscles turned to water. The desk came up and was about to hit his face. But nothing. It was cool. And he was unaware of his breathing.

The voice had lost its tinny ring. He could detect foreignness, but also a comforting timbre. It was a woman's voice. Not Sophia's.

—Charlie. Hi, I'm Dr Keshvardoust. Not feeling so good, hey?
—No.
—I can imagine. Well, it looks like you passed out, mate. You should start to feel yourself again within a couple of hours. We've given you something to keep you relaxed, but it might make you a little drowsy.
—I don't know what happened.
—It's okay. Have you been sick lately? Or stressed about something?
—No. Not sick. I don't know about — stressed.
—Okay. Well, your father is on his way. We'll all have a talk when he gets here.

Charlie lifted himself up in the bed. He was still hot, but the heat didn't have that escalating feeling. He looked at the doctor. She was a woman, not a girl; but she did have something girlish about her. Her hair, or maybe her eyes. He didn't hate her. In fact, he liked her. There was no sickening feeling like the one Sophia provoked in him. Oh, *Jesus*. Sophia. What the hell happened?

The doctor was talking to a family. A father, or maybe grandfather, and two girls. One of the girls was young, the other maybe his age. He liked the look of her too. She made him feel comfortable, not sick at all. In fact, the only thing left of that horrible feeling was the detaching memory of it. Charlie moved himself onto his side, and looked back at the girl. She was beautiful. She was with her family. Family. He wanted his father. It was the first time he'd wanted his father to be with him since — he couldn't remember the last time.

TWENTY-SIX

Sergeant Rosales checked the office for the third time for the return of his superior. The door was ajar. He was back. He could have rung the Senior Sergeant on his mobile, but thought it better to tell him in person. It was more bad news, or at least unsettling news. Now Sergeant Rosales wished he had called Testafiglia on his mobile. Despite the uncomfortable, sometimes even allergic, relationship he thought he had with his boss, Sergeant Rosales respected him. He didn't need this news; not now.

—Boss. How's the young bloke? Rosales asked.

—He's okay now. He's been under some stress, apparently.

—Oh. But it's all okay?

—Yes. How's everything here?

—Well, there's something you need to have a look at, Sergeant Rosales said, and produced the file from behind his back.

—What is it, Sergeant? Does it need my attention now?

Rosales put the fingerprint report on his boss's desk and slid it across to him.

Salvatore opened the report.

—Which case is this?

—One of the young rape victims. She called triple-oh yesterday saying that one of the attackers had contacted her and was on his way to her workplace. A patrol was sent but they were unable to locate him. He'd come to hand over a mobile phone to the victim — it had been stolen from her during the attack. We just got the report back from forensics. There's a partial print on it. Abdullah Najib. We'll have to get her in to ID him, but it looks like he's one of them.

—This is the same boy, isn't it? The little prick who broke my front window. Unbelievable. Oh, Jesus, Sergeant. Mia. My daughter.

—We'll pick him up, boss.

—Hang on. We've only got a partial print, right? This little arsehole won't agree to an ID parade, so we'll have to get the victims to look at some photos. We don't have to get all the girls down here at once — but as soon as one of them makes an ID we'll pick him up. Oh, and make sure that, ah — Patrick White — is in the photo array for all the girls other than the one who knows him.

—Done and done, Rosales replied, moving towards the door.

—Actually, this victim, the one who had the phone stolen, she said she'd gone with the boys to use an illegal substance, didn't she? Sergeant, get that White down here for more questioning. I believe he's still on probation, so we can bring him in. He admitted to knowing one of the other victims; see if he has any connection with this one. And if he's still dealing drugs he certainly won't be after this. Jose, I've had it up to here with this. Rapes, drugs. This is the suburbs — where families are trying to make a living and have a bloody home.

★

Tennille Baxter looked at the photos. They lacked the colour of real people. They wore expressions that could not be identified.

—That guy's eyes — maybe, she said tentatively, and rubbed her own eyes.

—You recognise this guy? Rosales prompted.

—I dunno.

—Take your time. It's okay.

Tennille had decided that she would go ahead with the charge if they caught them. But she wished the cops would just arrest the bastards. She didn't want this. She didn't want to have to look at photos, and especially not here, in this police station. The last time she was here was the night of the rape.

—Are these guys suspects? They don't even look like they're, you know, police photos.

—Well, Miss, we can't show you photos that suggest that the people in them have been under arrest. But we wouldn't show you any photos unless we needed to.

Tennille looked at them again. Several of the suspects were ethnic, and a few Anglo-Aussies. She pushed these aside. Then she noticed the slight smile on one of the remaining photos. It was the smile of the first guy.

—This guy, she said, he's not the one who had my phone, but he was one of them.

—This one?

—Yes. Well, I thin—

—Thank you, Miss Baxter.

TWENTY-SEVEN

—Abdullah Najib, you've been detained here at Western Plateau Local Patrol for the purpose of an interview. You can decline to answer our questions if you wish. You are not under arrest. My name is Sergeant Rosales. This interview will be videotaped. Do you understand?

—What's decline mean?

—It means it's up to you if you wish to answer our questions.

—Depends on what the questions are.

—Do you agree to the interview?

—I'll tell ya when I won't answer ya questions.

—Okay, Abdullah, can you tell me what you were doing on the twenty-sixth of May this year?

—Nuh. Don't keep a diary.

—Have you ever been to Rooty Hill Plaza?

—Dunno, maybe.

—Have you ever taken young women for a drive in your car? Young women you met at Rooty Hill Plaza?

—Plenty!

—So, yes?

—I guess, why?

—Have you ever smoked marijuana with young women and then propositioned them for sex?

—Maybe — nuh.

—Have you ever forced young women to perform acts of a sexual nature against their will?

—Ah — nuh.

—Okay, mate. Why don't you tell me what you did do with the young women you had in your car, then.

—Nuthin. If any chicks have said anything, they're bullshitting.

—But you're not?

—That's right.

—Well, we've got your mate next door. The boss is talking to him right now. What if he says differently?

—What mate?

—Your mate you score the drugs off.

Abdullah felt adrenaline jab through his veins. He hadn't thought of this. That they would bring in the other boys. My mate I score the drugs off? he thought. I don't score off nobody. It gets given to me. Fadi gets pot off the skips at his work since my cousin had to stop selling. Fadi's in there? Next door, being drilled too? That fucking cunt. He's already told them about the weed. He'll fuckin' tell them everything, the pussy.

—Look. We did take some chicks for a ride. But whatever they said happened, they wanted it. They knew.

—And what was it, Abdullah? What did they want?

—You know. Sex.

—So you did have sex with the young girls you met at Rooty Hill Plaza?

—Yeah. But they let us. They were sluts.

—Can you tell me their names, Abdullah?

—I dunno — Tenni, Melissa, those chicks?

—Okay, Adbullah Najib, I'm terminating this interview and informing you that you are now under arrest. You will be detained here at Western Plateau Local Patrol.

—Is Fadi under arrest too?

—Fadi who?

—My mate, you said is next door being questioned.

—His name isn't Fadi, but I think we should get this Fadi down here and ask him a few questions.

TWENTY-EIGHT

Whitey left the cop station and headed straight for Booze World. The fuckwits came to get him at work. The pigs actually came into the shop and told the boss they needed to talk to Mr Patrick Irvine White. It was close to knock-off time, but he'd still get docked for leaving fifteen minutes early. Whitey doubted he'd keep his job after this. Sacked 'cause the pigs were stupid, stupid fuckwits. Whatever the fuck that was, it had fuck-all to do with him. Going on and on about Natalie and some other chicks. Giving me a piss test. Asking about Lebanese blokes who I sell to. Same shit as last time. And some other crap about forcing women to have sex. For a second Whitey had feared that Sonja's parents were trying to have him charged. But the questions were too wide of the mark for that. The only worry was the piss test. He hadn't had a smoke for a few days, but it was probably still in his system. Well, they'd let him go for now. But the pricks wouldn't give any documentation to prove that they'd fucked-up. His boss'd never believe that he was innocent of whatever it was they'd pulled him out of work for.

He was close to tears, but turned them back inside to evaporate into anger.

It was a fair walk to Booze World, but Whitey was flying. He could already see the barn-style roof reflecting the whiteness of the twilighting sun over the grey-green suburb.

—Whitey, mate. Haven't seen you in donkeys, Agro said, slapping the counter with his meat-tray hands.

—Yeah. How ya been? Whitey asked. He felt better. He had friends in the drug and alcohol industry.

—Not bad, mate. Not bad. What ya after?

—Somethin' ta get wasted.

—That's the spirit. In fact, I've got just the spirit for it. Agro pointed to the floor stack of Wild Turkey. Twenty-four bucks fa you, mate.

—Sold. I'll get a couple a cans for the walk too, Whitey said, taking his hands out of his pockets and grabbing a bottle.

—So. Got a job? Agro nodded at Whitey's Greedos garb.

—Maybe not fa much longer.

—That good, hey?

He could hear the voices in his flat as he approached the door. Sonja's brother and sister were over again. He put his key in and turned the worn lock.

—Patrick, Sonja said. What happened? The police were looking for you.

—So you told them where I work? Whitey grunted and put the bottle on the kitchenette bench.

—Of course not. I did let it slip that you were at work. They asked me where you worked but I said I didn't know. They said they'd check with the Welfare Centre.

—I've told you, don't trust 'em.

—I'm sorry. But I didn't tell them, Patrick, I promise.

—Yeah, okay.

—So what was it about? she asked, and ran her fingers through her sister's hair.

—I have no fuckin' idea.

—Hello, Patrick, Polly said.

—Hi, Poll. Sorry for the bad language.

—Hello, Patrick, Peter said.

—Hi, Pete.

Whitey opened the bottle and poured a glass half full of bourbon. He added a dash of Coke.

Sonja turned toward her sister and whispered something. Whitey snarled and drank off the glass. He poured another.

—Let's go back home, Sonja said, and touched her brother's shoulder.

—Bye, Whitey waved.

Whitey put on Anthrax's *Among the Living* and poured another bourbon. He had to put the glass down and air-drum to the title track. He then air-guitared the verse riff and drank off the bourbon. Another was definitely in order. He drank it. He'd totally forgotten why he was drinking until Sonja came into view and turned down the stereo.

—Leave it, Sonja, he said, and stumbled up to increase the volume again.

—It's way too loud, Patrick.

—'Follow me or die', he said, complete with satanic hand sign.

—Patrick, settle.

—Don't be a bitch.

—Don't say that, Patrick. I'm not a bitch.

—Just let me listen to my music, okay?

—Why are you acting like this?

—Why do you think?

—I have no idea, Sonja replied, and turned down the stereo further.

—Because no matter what I do, the pigs come in and fuck me up. I mean, really, this time, I haven't done anything.

—Look, I'm sorry. But why are the cops always after you?

—'Cause I'm known.

—Will they ever leave you alone?

—I doubt it.

—It freaks me out a bit, Patrick. I mean, you're not bad, my dad's a much worse person than you are. But you can't seem to stay out of trouble.

—Yeah, well, this is their fucking trouble. Not mine.

—I don't think I can live with it, Patrick. The cops'll never leave us alone, will they?

—They'll never leave me alone.

—That's what I mean. I don't think I can live with it.

—Then go.

Sonja sat in front of the television, close, so she could hear it above the music. The dialogue meant nothing though. She'd never felt like this about Patrick. She'd never been angry with him. She hated it. She hated herself. She breathed deeply and tried to relax her tensed facial muscles.

—What? Whitey grunted at the old guy standing at his door.

—Jesus, Sonja said from behind Whitey.

Whitey turned to face her. He was at that stage of drunkenness where he was still aware of and comfortable with the slowness of his movements and reactions, and not afraid to cock his head, slowly, like a confused beagle.

—That's my — she began, and looked past Whitey to the man. Dad, what are you doing?

—Sonja. Is this him? Zakhar asked.

—What's going on, Dad?

—This is not right, Sonja. I think it is time things change back.

—What the fuck's goin' on? Whitey snarled. Is this ya dad?

—Yes, she replied.

Whitey tried to focus on the man. He had something of Sonja's eyes about him. Other than that, this man was totally foreign to him.

—Look, mate, Whitey said. This is not a good time. I've had a cun — I had a shit day today.

—I think Sonja should come back tonight, Zakhar said.

—Come back? Come back where?

—To her home.

Zakhar was suddenly in the flat. Whitey hadn't noticed him walk past. Sonja had just as suddenly sat down. The two were talking. Whitey couldn't think what he should do. His senses totalled tasting the bourbon coming back up his gullet. But in the next second he'd grabbed the man by the back of his shirt.

—Get out, Whitey growled.

Somewhere Whitey heard Sonja say *Don't*. And the room was murky. One of them slapped him. Across the cheek. Whitey pushed out blindly, and all three hit the carpet.

Whitey got to his feet as quick as if he were sober. Sonja was lying down, holding her shoulder. Her father had sat up.

Sonja had expected one of her parents to come to the flat eventually; they were virtually next-door neighbours, after all. She thought it would be her mum though. And if it ever was her dad, she assumed it would be because he was drinking again. He seemed sober. And most of all, he seemed strong. She felt herself loving him again, or even loving him for the first time, involuntarily, and painfully in her chest, and in a way she'd wished she could always love him. And then, like some stupid school drama production, all three players had crashed to the floor.

She'd hurt her shoulder. But the pain was nothing compared to the tsunami of emotions that had dumped her. Patrick looked too young next to her father. He looked like a kid who'd just tipped a fish tank onto the carpet. And her father. Who got up off the floor without looking like the rickety old drunk he usually did, and spoke evenly to Patrick.

—Sonja will come back with me tonight. We can talk tomorrow, or when you are sober.

—Dad, let me talk to him for a minute, she said.

She could tell that her words stunned Patrick. Far more than her father's slap to his face.

—Shut the door, Patrick ordered as her father walked out.

—Look, Patrick, she began. There must be something going on at home. Maybe I should go back with him.

—Home? Isn't this your home?

—Yes, but so is my parents' place.

—Oh. Piss off then. Go with 'im.

Whitey looked around the flat for the bottle after they'd left. He'd begun to think that Sonja's father had taken it with him until he found it on the stove, far more depleted than he thought it'd been.

TWENTY-NINE

Abdullah could hear his mother through the metal and reinforced-glass door. It pissed him off. She was goin' on and on in Lebanese about his cousins. How it was Dad's fault for not severing ties with his brother once they'd moved to Australia. Abdullah wished his cousin and uncle were here now. It was pretty mad to be in the lock-up. Proved toughness. But there was no one to share it with. And it was gettin' fuckin' old: just sittin' here, listenin' to Mum, and not knowin' what the fuck else was goin' down.

He'd been charged. Assault. Sexual Assault. Detaining Without Consent for Advantage. It'd all get sorted though. Once they'd listened to the full story. Surely these fuckin' pigs'll be able to see they were just fucks. They won't even tell him which chicks were sayin' shit about him. He didn't know the names of all the chicks he'd fucked anyway. Fuck. That sounds mad. He'd had so many bitches he didn't even know all their names. Surely these fuckin' Aussies'll understand: Aussie chicks are sluts. Ya fuck 'em, but don't marry 'em. Who'd marry a chick who all ya mates've been through too? Guess Aussie blokes have to, 'less they marry a wog chick.

A cop unlocked the door and opened it a little.

—Your mother wants to speak to you, mate, but we're going to have to take a statement off you first. You can have legal advice at this stage if you wish.

—What's legal advice? Abdullah asked.

—Obtain a solicitor, or call yours if you have one.

—Nah, I wanna tell youse my side.

—Won't be long, mate.

The cop smiled as he closed and relocked the door.

THIRTY

Whitey woke up on the floor. He looked over at the bed. It was empty. He sat up and looked at the clock. Nine-thirteen. It must be am. Shit, is it a weekday? Friday. Late for work. Did Sonja go to school? He couldn't remember much since arriving home from the cop station. Except the dim lighting in his flat (the ceiling bulb was still on), and a thick, numb feeling about Sonja. She was going to leave him. Or had left. He knew that much. Not from memory. From the atmosphere in the flat.

He got up and stripped off his dampish clothes. He stumbled into the shower because he'd been working long enough now for it to be an involuntary thing. The sliver of soap was having trouble penetrating the alcoholic sheen on his body. As long as it could hide the stink. He dressed in his unironed shirt and pants and crossed the vacant streets to Greedos.

The coffee made him nauseous. He headed out of the tearoom to go for a spew and saw Mr Hardy, who looked at his watch.

—Mr White. Everything all right?

—Yes. It's all sorted out. It was a mistake.

—What was a mistake? Mr Hardy asked, and swapped a handful of papers to his other hand.

—The police. You know. How they came here yester—

—No. I think you've made a mistake. Patrick, you'd better come up to the office, mate.

Whitey's nausea receded, but it left his brain and face on fire. There was ice in his legs though.

—I made my own inquiries with the police yesterday, Patrick, Tom Hardy said as he got behind his desk.

—Then you know it's a mistake.

—They told me you have a criminal record, Patrick. In fact, you've been incarcerated.

—Yeah —

—It's up to each store manager to make a decision about employing individuals with criminal records, Patrick, and I think, due to yesterday's little visit occurring during your probationary period, I'll have to let you go.

—Let me go? That's the sack, isn't it?

—It's the sack, yes.

—Should I go now, or do I have to work the rest of the day?

—You have to work the rest of the day.

But Whitey crossed back over the highway ten minutes later.

THIRTY-ONE

Sonja had felt strong all day. She'd felt more like a woman than she ever had before. But now, as she pulled the clothes out of the bag she'd brought from Patrick's flat back to her parents', she cried. Just tears and a shiver. But it was crying; and she hadn't felt it coming. It was just sad. Sad to think of him over there and herself here. Her clothes looked sad. She wiped the tears off her cheeks. Because he was probably drunk again. And it wouldn't be long before another visit from the police. But he would hug her now. And that was so important. *Jesus.* What had she talked herself into?

But there was no one else she could talk to but herself. Not her parents (they'd just tell her to forget him, come home), nor the other kids at school (they wouldn't know what the hell to say), nor her teachers (she still loved Patrick; she didn't want to get him into more trouble). But that was the problem. He was trouble. He didn't mean to be. But he'd always be in trouble. The only way he'd ever have any decent money would be from living just outside the line of trouble. It was the only way he'd ever known. They'd had money when he was selling drugs. Since he'd been working they'd been poor. He seemed to be able to handle it. But Sonja found it depressing. She'd never experienced anything beyond poor since her family had emigrated, and had never really expected to. And it wasn't the extra cash she and Whitey didn't have now so much as the loss of any spontaneity in their lives. It was just lean and boring. Except for him coming home drunk more often. Or bringing booze home. She could never imagine Patrick going back to school. She'd asked him a few times whether he'd consider going back to school. He didn't even realise you could complete high school as an adult. He'd laughed at it. And university; he'd said he didn't know exactly what that was. He would never have a good job. Or a well-paying job. And it wasn't because he didn't deserve it. Patrick was a good person. He was really the best person she'd ever met. But his life was the way it was. Sonja had absolutely no idea how she would go about changing Patrick, or even suggesting changes to him.

Sometimes she'd hear other girls at school talking. Talking about their boyfriends. Their boyfriends all sounded like kids. And it made her feel good to know that she had a man. But she'd also hear them talk about what their boyfriends did. University, apprenticeships, working toward things. And the plans — however shallow and probably unrealistic — that the girls would talk about made Sonja feel as if she'd missed a whole era of her life. As if her plans had been made — she'd decided to become an adult, at sixteen.

Moving back with her family presented itself as a fresh start for her. A clean page, with a sober father. And a clear mind. But it was going to be complicated, she could tell.

THIRTY-TWO

Mia sat in the interview room and found she had trouble breathing. She was nervous, but hadn't expected this level of anxiety. An officer came in, one she hadn't seen before when she'd been here with her father. Mia was thankful it was a female officer.

—Hi, Mia. I'm Constable Wong. Your father asked that I conduct this interview. As you probably know, he's removed himself from this case, and you also personally know a number of the other officers here, so it might not have been comfortable talking to them.

—Okay.

—So, we'll start at the beginning. How did you meet Abdullah Najib?

Mia told her. She told her everything she could remember. And it was like she was telling the story of some other girl. Especially now, since she'd heard bits and pieces of what Abdullah and his mates had done. That girl, that other Mia, was a fucking fool.

When she had finished, the officer asked her the names of all of Abdullah's friends, and if she knew where they lived. Mia could give their first names, at least most of them, but not exactly where they lived. Even when they'd gone to Abdullah's friends' houses, she couldn't say where they were, because she'd never driven, and most of the time the surroundings were unfamiliar to her.

—Abdullah and his friends lived around Punchbowl, which is a fair few suburbs away from Newington, right?

—That's correct, Mia.

—And you say they met these girls in the western suburbs?

—Yes.

—I heard them mention the west a few times, and then they'd laugh and give each other high-fives. I realise now that's what they must have been talking about.

—Okay. Now, Mia. Did Abdullah, or any of his friends, force you to have sex?

—Will my dad hear any of this?

—Yes, he may. But if you were raped, Mia —

—Abdullah and I had sex. He didn't force me —

—Did you use protection? A condom?

—He wouldn't.

—You need to have a blood test, Mia.

—Oh, Jesus. Oh no. I have been feeling sick.

—And if you're sure it was consensual, your father doesn't have to hear about it, Mia. But make sure you get that test. We can arrange it for you.

—Thanks —

Mia began to cry. Cry from real pain. That girl, the one she'd just told the story about, that other Mia, was her. She'd been foolish. She'd gone out with that arsehole. She couldn't picture it, the things he was supposed to have done. But then there was that time he hit her. That guy, that monster who'd hit her, he would be capable of anything. She was lucky he hadn't done it to her. Offered her up to all his ugly mates. How could her judgment have been so off? How could she not have seen what he was like? He'd broken her, emotionally. Mia couldn't bear to think about what he'd done to all those other girls.

THIRTY-THREE

Whitey could finally drink no more. Not even water. His stomach was rejecting everything. Everything was coming out. Sweat, tears, shit, vomit. He'd been drinking for a few days, trying to get used to the strange new flat. The flat without Sonja. It was empty. It smelt sweet, like rotten grapes or apples. Or both. He'd been able to take ownership of the Sonja-less flat while he was drunk. But the cement-rendered walls were cold this morning, reflecting the feel of this sudden sobriety. He got up off the floor. He showered, but the soap had finally been reduced beyond utility. He stood in the water through hot, warm and then dead cold. He shaved before drying off. His hands were steady, but his head was shaky. He threw all the clothes he could find into the twin tub and dressed in some jeans and a grey (once black) shirt, neither of which had been worn since before his stretch in prison. He headed out of the flat.

He climbed the stairs and knocked on the door. He knew he wouldn't have been able to do this in any other emotional or physical state. Not drunk. Not sober. But in this purgatory it was possible.

Sonja's mother answered.

—Hi, Whitey mumbled.

—Hello.

—Is, um, Sonja here?

—She's getting ready for school. I don't know if she wants to talk to you.

—Oh.

—I'll see if she will, Mrs Marmeladova said without looking at Whitey.

Sonja came through the lounge room to the door. Her hair was still a bit wet. She looked older. She didn't smile.

—Wait outside. I'll come out in a minute, she said.

When she did come out she smiled a little, he thought.

—Hi, Sonja.

—Hi, Patrick. How have you been? You look — pale.

—All right. Actually, not good, Sonja. I miss you.

—I miss you too, Patrick.

—Will you come back to me?

—I don't know, Patrick.

—Why did you go, Sonja? Don't you love me anymore? Suddenly he felt faint — as if the carpark they were in was suddenly not real; and neither was the blood pushing up to his head.

—It's not that. But things changed.

—What? What changed? Whitey asked, beginning to sweat and get a cold, tight feeling in his torso as blood and concrete rushed back to this new reality.

—Look, I love you, Patrick. I've never loved anyone else. But — the only way to say it is going to sound cold, but it's not. It feels like our relationship was a phase; a phase of my life. One I'll never forget. One that was perfect. But nothing perfect can last. Nothing lasts. Things change —

—It can be perfect again. I'll change if that's what it is, Patrick pleaded, and hated the sound of his voice.

—I don't want you to change. That's not it. Like I said, I don't think we can go back to how it was. I was so in love with you, nothing else mattered, and I loved feeling like that, but when it started to go, I saw that there are other things that matter.

—But I don't matter? Patrick asked.

—Of course you matter. We just need to take some time out, stop and look at what we're doing.

—So you'll come back? After some time?

—I don't know, Patrick. Maybe we'll be together in the future. But I think for now we should give it a break.

—For how long?

—I don't know. I've got to get going to school though. I'm late.

—Do you want me to walk with you?

—No. That's okay.

He watched her walk off. He'd never found her sexier. He grabbed his bottom lip between his thumb and forefinger and squeezed it until it really hurt. He tried not to cry and realised that he'd never fought against, or ever really cared about, a girl breaking up with him before. He'd always known that it would suck severely when he did finally give a shit. It was worse. But there was some hope to take away from this. Wasn't there?

THIRTY-FOUR

Salvatore almost walked out of the Pigeons Arms as soon as he walked in. He'd never had a drink by himself. But it was the only way, or at least the most painless way, he'd reasoned, he could digest what he had to digest. And to decide what to do about it.

He ordered his beer, carried it to a booth and had a couple of sips, then a long pull on the schooner glass. He took the plastic bag out of his briefcase.

Maybe it was his years of policing, or maybe it was the strength of his connection with his daughter — either way, something had forced him to look in the bin next to the upstairs toilet at home. Wrapped too obviously in half a roll's worth of toilet paper was a pregnancy test stick. Blue, faded, but nonetheless blue: positive. It couldn't be Maria's. She would tell him if she was pregnant. The second she knew. And Mia. She was, in hindsight, displaying signs. Nausea, increased appetite, crying. Salvatore had heard his daughter crying. Crying in a way he'd never heard her cry before. Not sulking or sooking. Crying like a woman. He'd reasoned it was because of the Abdullah Najib thing, but this had prompted him to think it was more. Constable Wong had told him that Mia had not been raped. But was Mia lying? Or had she slept with him? Or someone else?

The beer was working. He'd tried to take the plastic bag out of his briefcase at work after closing his office door. But the hot blood in his chest made him feel like vomiting. His mind searched for a way to make it not true. Here, with three-quarters of a glass of Tooheys in one hand, he could touch the open plastic bag. And begin to work through the sickening information. Because this luck was his; he'd have to take ownership. It was just like the sort of luck experienced by other people in the community he policed. But never him. Did they feel like this? Did the parents of the many pregnant teenagers he'd seen in the suburbs of the Western Plateau go through this churning of emotion and partially digested penne lisœ? He'd never considered that they would. He'd thought that their bad parenting was to blame for unwanted pregnancies. So was he a bad parent? And just as important, was this pregnancy unwanted?

He drank off the rest of the beer. He wrapped up the plastic bag and picked it up off the table. He could still feel the nasty, hard little stick inside it. Salvatore got up to leave, but as he looked to the exit he realised he hadn't made any decisions.

He ordered another beer. And a blast of Galliano.

There was so much to consider. Just as he'd grasp some sort of answer, contingencies flew in from left field to topple his resolve. Like in discussing it with Mia, should he involve his wife? Would Maria complicate the situation or help? She'd have to know. Eventually. But should he tell her straight away? His instinct was not to. Salvatore had kept a strangle-hold on his emotions over this, and was beginning to feel almost proud of himself. He wanted to deal with this situation while he still had a good grip. Maybe Maria would make him, or let him, let go.

Driving helped his thoughts run a bit smoother. He'd come to a decision. At least, the forward motion of the car had let him fix on one. He would talk to Mia. Not confront, talk. He wouldn't even produce the evidence. It was, after all, something very private. Something his daughter had had to dip in her own urine — and quite desperately. And he wouldn't make her confess. What she'd done wasn't criminal. It was something more confronting to Salvatore at this moment. What she'd done was human.

The poles of Salvatore's world had been reversed. He was a passionate man. But he'd always saved his passion for his home life. At work, he'd never let his emotions rule. You can't. You simply cannot as a police officer. That's why he was where he was today — with his own patrol. But last night he'd brought some of that professionalism into his home. He'd acted like a cool-headed, professional father. If there was such a thing. But his emotions needed aspirating. And he was at work now, with much entrusted power at his disposal. And he'd forgiven more than he was ever prepared to forgive.

So he made the call, while it was still hot inside him. To an old mate who'd moved over to Corrective Services. Long Bay *Jail*. A call to ensure the future would hold some satisfaction.

THIRTY-FIVE

The worst part is when you wake up every morning. And see the walls. And the stupid fuckin' metal toilet with no seat. Sleep was perfect though. While you were in it. But the others in here, and the guards, don't give a fuck about keepin' the noise down. Abdullah had built a place he could get to in deep sleep. And every second spent there was warm and quiet and soft. But the dreams he had to travel through to get there were fucked. Traps. Traps that could keep you bound up until some cunt woke you by yelling or coughing or banging something. You were thankful to get out of the trap, but pissed off you didn't get a chance to break through to the deep place.

The guard slid the door open.

—Shower, mate.

And in the open shower area he saw what he'd been expecting to see every day since he'd been refused bail. One of his mates. They looked at each other. Abdullah nodded slightly and wondered if it was the right thing to do. Fadi was naked. He had a pretty small cock. Everyone in here did. Even him. Abdullah hated the showers. It was typical, he thought, that of all places he'd see Fadi at the showers.

—Hey, Abdullah said.

—Hey.

—So. You're in here, Abdullah continued, and almost began to undress, but shifted from one foot to the other instead.

—Yeah. They hammered me, mate.

—So are we mates?

—Yeah, I guess. Why? Fadi asked and tried to cover his cock with the soap.

—Dunno. I just been thinkin' I ain't got no mates since I been in here.

—We done the same thing, mate, Fadi said and put a towel between himself and the awkwardness of the situation.

—But what did we do? Abdullah asked.

Fadi quickly dressed to avoid answering Abdullah. He too wondered what they'd done. It was so remote — and doubly so in here — from his life now.

—Dunno, he shrugged.

The Bellevue Remand Centre dining hall was small but the sound of coughs and snorted phlegm ricocheted off the ecru brick walls. Abdullah had no appetite for the cold toast and cereal but had learned to force it down. He was starting to feel skinny. And Fadi seemed bigger now, so Abdullah would try not to leave a crumb of the dry Aussie food today.

—Do ya talk to anyone in here? Fadi asked.

—Nuh. No cunt's in here for more than a few months, I think, so no one really talks. Some cunts do. But not to me.

—What'd ya get charged with? Fadi said.

—Rape and some shit.

—Same.

—Rape. I never thought it was rape, man. Sluts are sluts. It's well-known, isn't it? Abdullah said and tossed his neck until the vertebrae cracked satisfyingly.

—I can't work it out. I never thought any of this shit would happen. I thought we'd get in shit for takin' that chick's mobile. I didn't think she'd go tellin' anyone about what we did. I mean, why would a chick want to tell people about that?

—Fuckin' bitches. That fuckin' Mia give me up to her father, too.

—What about the little brother, that Charlie fucker? Fadi asked.

—I don't know what ta do about him. I told my solicitor that a pig's son was involved and he told me to leave it with him, not ta mention it ta any cunt yet.

—Did ya olds get a Leb solicitor for ya? Fadi asked.

—Nuh. Some fuckin' Turkish cunt. At least he's Muslim.

—I got a Leb. But the prick wanted to know every fuckin' thing. He says I'll probably do some time.

—Mine says that too, Abdullah replied. You know, now, since bein' in here, when all ya can do is think and shit, it's like that whole time we were with those chicks I was someone else. Like I handed the wheel over to some other cunt. And they just floored it.

—Yeah, I know what you mean, man, Fadi said. But we did do it. Man, I never told ya, but each time we did it I got this shit feeling after, and it kept getting worse each time. Did you get that feeling too, man? And ya kept remembering the look on the chicks' faces. Did you get that too?

—Yeah. I got it. Lookin' back, I got it. But a lot of things make me feel shit. Man, we gotta stick to sayin' that the chicks wanted to go with us, wanted to fuck us, okay?

—Yeah, I know. My solicitor says the same thing.

PART THREE

THIRTY-SIX

The school had such a different feel at night. Charlie liked to get there a bit early for his lesson and take in the atmosphere. The corridors in cool, inviting darkness, the vinyl tiles and plaster ceiling silent, the classrooms in stasis. There were kids who'd pay-him-out for coming to an extra lesson, out of school time; but he wouldn't miss these lessons for anything.

He'd started learning guitar. It had come out of him seeing a psychologist, after he had fainted that day at school. He hadn't told the psychologist about him and Abdullah, but she knew he was stressed and highly anxious about something, and needed to escape it. She didn't press him too much. But she did suggest that he get involved in something outside of school — sport, a youth group. Neither of these sounded like they'd help him. But he'd seen an MTV special on Black Sabbath guitarist Tony Iommi when he was still off school sick. He'd never heard of him, but something about the guy — his non-rockstar, relaxed attitude, the cool way he stood on stage and delivered lightning-fast solos, and the fact that he was of Italian heritage, but not uptight and traditional like his father — impressed him. Iommi had lost the tips of his fingers in an industrial accident, but had developed a way to play with plastic caps on them, inadvertently pioneering, a whole genre of music. Charlie had never really thought about playing an instrument, but it was in his head now. He asked his parents to buy him a guitar, an electric one, for his birthday. They said he had to have lessons though, and when he found out his father had enrolled him in these classes — at his school — it was a bit of a downer. Until the first lesson. They were one-on-one and James, the guitar tutor, was cool. But like Tony Iommi, he didn't look it. He was old — thirty-something, maybe even forty — had long hair, and smelled like tobacco and marijuana smoke. But man, he could play! And he didn't laugh or pay-out when Charlie couldn't get it right; he'd say good, good, man, that's almost it. He'd been a professional musician in the eighties, and had cool stories about life on the road in a rock band that, although he said they were hard years, sounded like the best times ever. Constant pranks, and travel, and insane characters who could only exist in the rock music scene. And he told Charlie that music is a religion, and that the school, a Catholic school, wouldn't let him teach if they knew he'd said that, but that he'd know when he got the religion: he'd feel it as part of himself, and he'd have faith. It blew Charlie away. Because after only a few months, he was really starting to feel it.

He looked forward to the new songs he'd learn every week with busting anticipation. James had said to bring along any music he wanted to learn and he'd teach it to him, but Charlie decided to leave it up to James. It was so much cooler to learn a song that he knew James loved. Van Halen, Led Zeppelin, Deep Purple, and of course Black Sabbath — all these old bands, they had unsurpassable music. Charlie couldn't believe no one he knew listened to them anymore. And learning the songs was like discovering a new part of yourself.

James came into the music room. He was always late.

—Hey, bro, how ya been?

—Good, thanks, James.

—All right, have I got a song for you, he said, unpacking his '74 Les Paul. Charlie had decided he'd buy one of those instead of a car in a few years.

—Yeah? Cool.

—Metallica! But this isn't no thrash metal song. This is a masterpiece.

—Is it hard?

—It's all in the feel. Once you get that, you'll kill it. It's called 'Nothing Else Matters' and mate, tonight, and when you practise it this week, nothing else will matter. It's a two-guitar piece, but I'll teach you both parts and you can improvise.

James was right. It was all in the feel. The main passage was quite simple — mostly open strings with minimal fret-work, but it was intense. And the accompaniment is perfect. Light trills that fitted into it, but change it quite dramatically. They jammed to it until Charlie got the feel, and then James sang the lyrics. He sang it with a tenor Charlie hadn't heard him use before, and the words, clear and powerful, seemed to make James tear up a bit. They had to stop because Charlie lost concentration. He looked down at the guitar, embarrassed — to see James like that, and for his own sloppy fingering.

—You okay, man? Sorry, did I freak you out? James asked him, the notes still ringing out.

—Um, nah, I just lost it a bit there.

—That song gets to me, man, sorry. Takes me back to a time, you know? I used to have a girlfriend, Aimee, we were together for a few years. She got breast cancer, man, and it eventually killed her.

—Oh. I'm sorry.

—But, you know, man, what makes it even worse is I treated her pretty poorly when we were together. Didn't respect her. I used to take a lot of drugs and booze, not come home, play around with other girls. Took her for granted, you know. Never got to make it up to her.

Charlie ran his hand along the neck of his guitar. He'd been able to put what he'd done to those girls right at the back of his mind, particularly when he was at guitar lessons, but here it was, at the forefront. He could relate all too well to what James was talking about. About disrespect.

—You okay, man? I did freak you out, didn't I?

—Nah. Well, a bit. But it's me. I've done some bad stuff, really bad stuff to girls too. Forced them. Made them do stuff, you know? Me and these guys I hung 'round with.

—And you feel bad about it?

—Yeah.

—Look, I don't want to know what you did, but it's good that you've realised it was a fucked thing to do — excuse the French — and you know how it feels to live with that. Man, respect the women in your life now. It won't make what you did go away, but you can make the rest of your life a better place. Sorry, man, I don't want to be preachy.

—Nah, James. Thanks.

Later at home, Charlie sat on his bed, noodling the licks he'd learnt earlier on his guitar. He glanced at the mirror. The guitar looked pretty cool. It was only a knock-off of an Explorer, and the top E kept going out, but it made him look like a pro. He didn't like to make eye contact with the guy playing it, though. Tonight's lesson had really dug-up the things he'd done to those girls. James was right. He had to live with it. At least he was sure there was no way he'd ever do anything like it again.

He'd done it because he'd been afraid of girls, or at least unconfident and nervous around them. He thought that with Abdullah, he'd get over that. He'd be the one making the girls nervous. But it had made it worse. Much worse. He still felt terrible when he was around girls — and women. And he didn't like touching them, or them touching him. Even his mum and sister.

It had gotten a bit better, since that day he'd passed out at school. He hoped now that his guilt would translate into respect. Because he would respect women now. And he would pray that it would help erode those feelings of self-loathing over what he'd done. But did he deserve his guilt to be worn away?

THIRTY-SEVEN

Abdullah had found it a relief to be in protection when he'd first arrived at Long Bay to begin his twenty years. It was a relief to be away from all the skip convicts, and not to have to look at their heads all day like he was forced to do in remand. But after a few weeks he realised it was an added punishment. Where on the outside he'd been a leader, a gang leader, defined by his relationship with others, in here there was nothing. No relationships. Except with the guards. And they led him. And mostly ignored everything he said.

The guard led him to a different yard for his morning exercise.

—They're doin' some work in protection yard this morning, he explained.

This yard was small. You'd be lucky to fit a car in it. And it was all concrete. No grass — nowhere to exercise, even if he wanted to. The only open part was the roof, which was caged over, about six metres up. He heard the gate shut and latch, and looked back. The guard had gone back in, but there was a guy standing just to the right side of the gate. Abdullah hadn't noticed him coming in. He looked like an Abo. Big bloke.

—Howyagoin'? the guy grunted at him.

—Yeah, okay.

—Got ya in protection, hey?

—Yeah.

—Wha' for?

—Why? Abdullah asked. This didn't seem right. He'd seen a couple of guys out in the protection yard once or twice, but they hadn't spoken to him. They hadn't even looked at him, really. He assumed they were in protection too, and were told not to talk to any other inmates. This conversation, although he'd been craving dialogue, made him very uncomfortable. It was too full-on to go from nothing straight to this.

—What's ya name then, mate? the big guy asked.

—Najib. Abdullah Najib.

—So this is you, hey.

—Heard of me, huh. What's your name?

—Pete. Pete Crawford. Remember it. Not that it'll do ya any good. See, I'm from H Block. Not even meant to be here.

—What? What are ya doin' here then?

—Passin' time. Same as you. So, what they stitch ya up for?

—I dunno, mate. Why does it matter to ya?

—Don't wanna talk about it? 'S up to you.

—What are you in for? Abdullah asked him.

—You know the story. Some bullshit charge. I'll be out shortly though. Doin' the screws a favour.

—Yeah?

—Yeah —

Abdullah saw the guy's foot move forward so quickly he thought there'd been a lightning flash in the grey sky overhead. And then there was snapping in his top teeth, and the wall behind him was running him to the ground face first.

—Get up, he heard. And he realised what was happening. There was no pain though. *Just* a grinding sensation. He started to get up, not because he'd been told to — it was automatic. The yard seemed low and dull and he could hear the air around him blowing with force through his head. The Abo guy was there, and then Abdullah was aware that his jaw was against the wall, and he could see the guy thrusting, and feel the constant knuckles on the other side of his jaw.

The air was deafening. But for the crunch.

THIRTY-EIGHT

Sonja was loving her newly discovered creativity. She wasn't attending school anymore, but neither was she wasting her time. She'd done a test at TAFE, and had been assured that by the end of only one year of study, she'd be able to matriculate early anyway. She'd been writing, reams and reams of poetry, and stories that were linked by the common thread of pain and love. Her father, her mother, her siblings, and Patrick all inspired her now. There was so much pain and love. But mostly, she drew inspiration from herself. She was growing. It was terrifying when she'd first become aware of it, but now she couldn't wait for the future.

Sonja took a seat at the front of the bus and opened a yellowed copy of Strindberg's *Miss Julia*. She was reading, but drifting off occasionally, and thinking about Patrick. Everything she read made her think of him. There was always a character that resembled him in some way. Or was it just that these writers could charge a link in her mind that made her relate too deeply? She looked down at the pages and was soon back in the Count's kitchen and the struggle within. No, she thought, turning the stiff page, Patrick lacks *Jean's* manipulative edge. Sonja shifted her backpack off the seat next to her as the bus began to fill. Distracted, and beginning to feel a little nauseous, she looked at the other passengers. Did everyone suffer the same confusions? Did they all have the same strong, but sometimes pointless and directionless will to live? Do they all fear death? This was starting to become an obsession with Sonja. She'd become awfully aware of her own mortality lately. It was something she'd never really considered before. Sure, she knew she would one day die, but it'd never really triggered deep thought. These days, no matter how much she tried to dismiss her fear of death — because it wasn't really healthy for her, especially now — it would just pop into her head when it was the furthest thing from her mind. It was the balance, she'd decided. Between life and death. There was so much life going on inside her that her subconscious felt the need to balance things out. And she valued her life more than ever now. Because it wasn't just hers.

She worried about love too. She would have the love for and from her baby, and of course that would be more than enough. But there was another kind of love, and she'd been spoiled. She had never felt anything as intense as the thing she'd had with Patrick. And she was afraid she'd never experience that again. And it hurt. Her relationship with Patrick had died. Everything dies. But do things have to die so young? Patrick would always be a part of her life but, she'd discovered, unlike what the Christian religions would have you believe, resurrection is a myth. She'd tried to picture life with Patrick again, after she'd found out she was expecting, but she couldn't find the feelings that would bond her sufficiently to him. If a love dies, even if you do bring it back, it has to have prosthetics, or even life-support to keep it going. The damaged parts can be hidden, but the surgeons responsible will always know. People go on, but are they really happy? Maybe she was too young, and

Patrick was her first love, but still, she'd had near anxiety attacks thinking that she would end up sad and virtually devoid of romantic love. Like all the adults she knew. She was sure her parents didn't love each other the way she and Patrick had. Since her father had come back from hospital, they'd seemed to have found an easy tolerance for each other though, Sonja had noticed.

She'd dreaded telling them that she'd fallen pregnant. But her mother's pessimism had cushioned the blow.

—We were expecting it, Sonja, she'd said. We knew it would happen, as soon as you took off with him, we knew.

There was no yelling or arguing or high emotion. In fact, her father had not said a word about it. Still hadn't, to her. She didn't want to push him to talk, but she was uncomfortable not knowing exactly how he felt. Until a couple of weeks after Sonja had told them, she'd heard her parents talking together, quite cutely, Sonja thought, about how exciting it would be to have a baby around again.

Her parents had started treating her like an adult, she supposed. And she was an adult now. Her childhood was gone. Not that she'd really enjoyed it. But it was most definitely gone. And it did make her a little angry. At herself, at her parents, and at Patrick.

She really would have to find something else to occupy her mind on the bus. The trip's momentum was too conducive to introspection: this was the second time she'd nearly missed her stop. On the trip back she would begin a cycle of poems concerning death, she quickly decided.

At the clinic, which she'd decided at the beginning to visit on her own rather than suffer her mum's cynicism or Patrick's clumsiness, she took a seat and exchanged smiles with the other young women. There was only one other really young woman there, but Sonja had never talked to her. She seemed a bit stuck up. And she always came with a cop, probably her father. Sonja felt a wave of nausea. She hated the sight of them. She'd caught this from Patrick. Lucky she hadn't brought him. He would've ended up in the cop's cuffs somehow. Or at least made it obvious that he was a small-time crim.

Sonja smiled to herself. What a strange person he was for her to have fallen in love with. Once. They had nothing in common. Not that you have to share everything in a relationship, she was sure, but to be so different; it was a freak of nature. This baby must have really wanted to come into the world. Because what else would have brought her and Patrick together in such an intense way?

As the midwife entered the room, Sonja was sure that once her baby was born, much of her confusion would disappear. Wouldn't it?

THIRTY-NINE

You had to be adaptable. As a police officer, you had to be able to negotiate change, and know when and how to initiate it. But stubbornness was also an essential quality. If things changed too much, they could quite easily become unpredictable and unmanageable. Salvatore didn't like change. Not when he hadn't initiated it. And he was famous, even admired, for his immovable stance on certain things at the Western Plateau patrol. But he'd been surprised at how he'd adapted to this big shift in his life. He'd never considered, or never realistically considered, that he'd have a pregnant teenage daughter. To even think about such a situation would've caused sharp pain in heart and mind alike. But here he was, here his family was, dealing with it.

After Salvatore had told his daughter he knew she was pregnant, there had been a cyclone of emotions. How could Mia have done this? How could she have slept with that thing? Because it was him. How could she have been so stupid, and then so doubly stupid not to have protected herself? The betrayal. And then realising that his daughter was suffering. Badly. Not just crying because she was in trouble with her parents, but anguishing over how her life had been slammed onto an unexpected path. In the eye of the storm, Salvatore and his daughter had been able to discuss the various implications. Mia didn't want to abort the baby. She said she could not put herself through further immorality. Salvatore agreed, and despite the gravity of the situation, was proud that his daughter felt this way. It meant his parenting had had an impact on her. But he did say that he would support her if she decided to seek the alternative. She wasn't sure if she would keep the baby; if she could love it. But she would rather live with that. The storm raged on, but passed, and with the exposed emotions it left in its wake, the family started to negotiate their new life. And the weekly ritual of the three of them — father, mother and daughter — attending the clinic came to mean more than its actual necessity.

FORTY

He'd be a skinny little shit for the rest of his life. That's what one of the guards had said. He'd told the guard to go fuck himself, or tried to, but he couldn't deny that it was true. Abdullah could feel the weight evaporating off him daily. The food in jail was shit enough, but this liquefied shit was the worst. His jaw would never work again; that's what the doctor cunt had told him. And that was true too. It'd been reattached, but the cunts hadn't done it properly. It just hung there. He could talk, if he rested the useless thing on his chest and forced his top lip to do all the work, but none of these arseholes wanted to listen to him anyway.

—Can't understand ya, all the guards snickered.

Fadi, who he'd seen in the prison hospital, had had six ribs broken in a fall down some stairs and been transferred out to Silverwater Correctional, where Ali was doing his time. And Abdullah was now in protection even from all the other pricks in protection. He'd told them the name of the guy who'd attacked him, but they'd informed him later that that prisoner was in a totally separate wing of the jail, and that he'd been released the day after the attack, and that Abdullah had obviously got the name from where it had been scratched into the wall of his cell. It was true. He'd never noticed it, but the name was there. Pete Crawford 11/9/99. His attack had been denied. He'd injured himself while in a rage, is how it was documented.

He interacted with only one other person now. His mother visited once a week. It hurt so much to see her. Way more than when his jaw had been bounced between knuckle and concrete. Because he'd become aware that he'd hated his parents, when they'd always loved him. His uncle and cousin had not come to the trial, and never came to visit him. Had totally disowned him. He looked forward to his mother's visits; he looked forward to that pain. He could talk to her way better than when his jaw had worked; like when he was a kid. She could make him laugh with her silly little stories, about when she was a girl in Lebanon. And it hurt to hear them. Because at the back of his mind was the knowledge that she would be gone again, and the stories would echo in him. And taunt him: he would never really laugh again. Never really enjoy anything. And never be able to get rid of the anger and frustration inside him. He would not physically be able to do so in here. So his mind was left to boil.

It wasn't Wednesday, when his mum visited, but he was led to the visitors' room. Abdullah's body rushed with hot, painful blood, and his mouth dried instantly when he saw the person sitting at the table.

She'd been in court a couple of times during his case, but he'd never looked directly at her. He wouldn't have known what expression to give her. He didn't hate her. But he didn't like to think about her. And seeing her here killed. He sat down, shakily, like an old man, or a spastic. The guards had put a pad and pencil on the table.

—Hello, Abdullah, she greeted him.

—Hi.

—They told me you can't talk properly, or it hurts you to talk, so I won't ask you anything.

—Okay, he said, and he felt like this situation was moving much too fast for him, like he was falling; and he felt like he was about to piss himself.

—I'm pregnant. To you.

—Oh.

—And all this stuff. It's virtually killed my parents, Mia said, and her eyes started to water. But she continued. They're going to help me. I just want to tell you one thing. These lies you've told about Charlie, trying to get him implicated in that sick shit you did. When your child is born, I will bring him to the jail to visit. If his uncle Charlie is in jail, he's the only person he will be visiting. Ever. It's up to you.

Abdullah grabbed the pad and pencil. His heart was beating, not so much fast, but hard, making his hand tremble. Mia looked so good. She was big. He didn't know about pregnancy, but he doubted she could get much bigger. She seemed to have put on a few kilos on top too. She looked good but. He did know that he wouldn't be able to fully grasp this situation now. It would have to wait until later, in his cell, when the blood had cooled. Alone. But nevertheless he tried.

He wrote on the pad: IS It a BOY.

—Yes. He's a boy.

He wrote under his previous letters: CaN I See HIM.

—Think about what I've said, Abdullah.

Mia left. She'd changed. So fuckin' much. He'd changed her. Changed her into something much stronger than the thing he'd changed into. It was a weird situation. He felt bad, but good; full, like he could burst. Burst into tears or something. And it was good to have a full head in here. You could lie there and lay it all out above you. And pick through it. And try things on in your head, and see if they felt right.

FORTY-ONE

Whitey opened another beer, his fourth, and drank off a good third in one slug. It wasn't touchin' the sides though. He'd been workin' it off — sweatin' it off — as soon as it hit his liver. It seemed he couldn't get anyone to help him move his stuff from Brunei to the new joint for all the piss in the world. So he'd started moving it — and drinking all the piss — himself. He didn't have much stuff to move, and this was a good thing, he supposed, but it was a little depressing. Twenty-seven years of stuff all fit into two trips in the Commodore. He could leave the handbrake off and lose the lot. Ah, well. Together they'd get good stuff. Eventually.

They'd rented a little house, half-house really, in Mt Druitt. It was a private rental, not Housing Commission, and this alone made him feel free. But even more, it was a fresh start. And with everything in her name they wouldn't have the cops knocking on the door looking for the old White scapegoat. He drank off another third and finally felt the effects as he surveyed his new home. He'd have a couple more and then do something with his stuff. Before she got back.

They'd decided that he'd sell — just to friends — to make a little extra cash so he could stay at home and study for his distance education HSC. He'd looked over the booklets they'd sent him. There was a whole bunch of shit he didn't understand, but he was looking forward to it in a way. She'd be able to help him with some of the stuff anyway. He was also pretty sure that if he finished the course, he'd be the first one in his family to get his HSC. Not that any of them would ever know about it. But still, it made him feel good to think about it. And of course there was someone else — someone special — who would be proud of him, and that was the best part of all.

Whitey shoved as much of his stuff as he could into the built-in wardrobe, and the rest he piled in a corner of the spare bedroom with his furniture. Her stuff, that her mum had given her, was much nicer. He'd get rid of all his old junk when he got around to it. But for now it could be shut up behind the spare bedroom door.

She came in with some groceries. She always had some sort of treat for him lately when she'd been to the shops. A Kit-Kat or Smarties. It made him a little uncomfortable, because he supposed she wanted him to do the same for her, but he just never thought of it when he was out. And the only shops he really went to were bottleshops, and he was pretty sure she wouldn't appreciate a can of bourbon and Coke that he'd end up drinking at least half of.

—Ya didn't get that stuff from Greedos, did ya? Whitey said, helping her get the bags onto the bench.

—No. Don't worry. I promised I wouldn't go there. I know how you feel about it, she said in mock frustration.

—Cool. Like a beer, babe? he offered, grabbing another for himself.

—I'd love one. It's so fuckin' humid out there. And if you've got some gear ready, I'd love a cone too.

—Sure, babe. I just mulled up earlier. Whitey stopped pouring her beer and went to get the bowl and bong from the lounge room cabinet.

After his second cone Whitey began to feel the tension tingle out of him. For some reason he'd been anxious for her to come home. This would be their first real night in the house together. He'd stayed the night she'd moved her stuff in, but he'd spent the last two back at Brunei Court, convincing himself that this was the right move by boxing up all his stuff. There was no turning back now. He was all here. But he needed her presence to make it real, he guessed. And as her expression suggested right now, she was reading his thoughts.

—So. How do you feel? All right about the whole thing?

—Yeah, Whitey replied. It's all good.

—It'll be weird, though. When the baby comes. Us living together now. Won't it?

—I dunno. Why? he asked and grabbed his beer.

—Will she mind you bringing it, sorry he or she, here?

—I dunno, Nat. I doubt it. She knows we're together.

—Yeah, but now we're living together, you know, it's —

—Look. I dunno. It's her problem if she's got a problem with it. She reckons she doesn't. That's all I have to go off.

And Whitey believed Sonja. She really didn't seem to have a problem with him seeing Natalie. She'd seemed happy for him when he'd told her — the day she'd come to tell him about the baby. And when he'd gone to see Sonja the next day to say that he wanted to marry her — that he still loved her — she'd hugged him, but didn't kiss him, and said that it was not what she wanted.

And *Jesus*, it hurt. He'd had to become like a wild animal, masking a trauma with normal, or normalish, behaviour. He hoped that this move would help bury it.

—Okay. Sorry. I'll drop it. I know you don't like to talk about it. It's just — I dunno, weird, Natalie said.

—Life's weird, he replied with a shrug.

Natalie had pretended she was okay after she'd been assaulted. And she had convinced even herself until the fuckers were caught. She agreed to go ahead with the charges. Nothing would stop her doing that. But all the fear, the confusion, the mistrust of people, and of herself had come back. Meeting the other girls, despite the shock of what they'd been through, had helped. The sick thing they had in common bonded them, and went a little way towards the healing. If there was any. The prosecution team had been as understanding as they could be, but what they couldn't do was take away the fact that the pricks were there, and were free to look at the girls and talk to their solicitors and act as though they were humans who deserved fairness. The Rape Crisis women were there — and they at least knew fully well what the girls were experiencing. Seeing those pigs. Not only in court, but on the telly, and in the paper. It seemed like it would never fucking end.

In her statement she'd given Whitey's name, and the defence solicitor had tried to use the fact that she'd had a relationship with him to demonstrate that she was involved with criminals. It was mute. The fuckers had nothing. No real defence, and nearly got what they deserved. That is, if they get fucked in jail.

After it was over she went to see Whitey. He'd heard about it and was pretty freaked out. But he didn't ask her too many questions, and listened to what she did tell him without a hint of the macabre interest that a couple of her other friends had shown. They'd hugged, and he held her for a long while. It was the first time she'd let a man touch her since the rape. She kept thinking about him. How he was, in his own strange way, and as much as a man can be, a feminist. He had none of the macho showiness or stupid sexual innuendo that the other guys she knew threw around. He was sensitive about what she'd been through, but didn't dwell on it and constantly ask her if she was okay. He'd once told her that he'd grown up without his dad, and had had to help look after his little sister. Maybe, she thought, the experience had done something to him. Given him an understanding that, she was sure, he was unaware of, but one that she could feel comfortable with. She'd started to visit him more often, and found herself feeling much stronger about him than she ever had before. Before she was assaulted. The fact that he'd just broken up with a girl — who he'd gotten pregnant — did give her some anguish, but she'd decided she needed Whitey. He was the man who could help her get over this and have a life again. And she thought she could help him.

—Hey, Nat said, I saw Tennille today. You know, the girl from my court case. She's just started back at her old job at the cinema and she said anytime we want to see anything she'd let us in for free.

—Cool, Whitey replied. This was much more comfortable than talking about Sonja. Anything you wanna see?

—I dunno. Maybe we could just go down and check what's on. I like her. She's heaps cool, Tennille is.

—Sure. Whatever you wanna do, babe.

So they finished their drinks and had another cone each to prepare themselves for the crowds at the cinemas. They were about to leave when Nat stopped and asked him the inevitable question.

—I just want to ask you one thing, Patrick. And then I swear I'll drop it.

—What?

—Is there any chance you would want to get back with Sonja after the baby's born? I mean, have you really thought about it?

—Fuck, Natalie. Yes. Yes, I've thought about it. And no. There's no chance. She made that clear.

—She made it clear. But what about you? Will you want to get back with her?

—No, Natalie. No way, he said firmly.

But he had to harshly cut and quickly shape the words from the truth. Because the honest answer to her question was Fuck yeah. In a western Sydney second.

OUT WEST

FORTY-TWO

Whitey parked his lorry two streets away from the school and legged it the rest of the way to the gate. It was futile to try and do battle with the polished four-wheel drives that congested the street Plumpton Primary was on. Wednesday was his day to pick up his daughter, to spend some time with her.

The bell the children had been hanging out for since lunch sounded, and the clamour to exit began. Whitey mooned around at the gate, aware of his maleness. He couldn't remember parents crowding the gate of the school when he was a young bloke, but it seemed the custom now. Kids, not all that anxious to be enclosed into the family off-roaders, began their games cut short by the end of their lunch break.

—Spot the bloody Aussie, isn't it? said a guy standing next to Whitey.

Whitey smiled and nodded at the guy — initially comforted that he wasn't the only bloke there picking up his kid. He looked in the direction that the guy pointed. At the multiculturalism that was truly at work in a game of handball. The kids were intent on the ball and its trajectory inside the hand-drawn court, perfectly oblivious of their variegated ancestries.

—There was none a that goin' on when I was a nipper, the guy continued. I never even seen an Arab or a Nip 'round 'here when I was growin' up.

Whitey smelt the sweetness of the guy's beery breath, and a pang of envy sped through him. He wished he was able to be drunk at three in the arvo but he couldn't risk a middy because of his job.

He saw his daughter coming towards him — a tiny version of Sonja. She was hand-in-hand with her best friend, Tuyen. The western suburbs his daughter had inherited were unlike the ones Whitey had grown up in. The Commission estates Whitey had known were being sold off and levelled and transformed into uniform manors. There was a drive to be middle class in the west that was lost on Whitey but he did hope that his daughter would learn some of it. Not so much so she would have material success, but so she would have an understanding of how her world operated. There was little hope for Whitey and the bloke standing next to him; they'd be left behind. Even the once benevolent government was cutting their ilk loose into the increasingly free market economy at every opportunity. Not that any of this really bothered Whitey. I'm a lucky bastard, he thought as he hugged his daughter hello.

They piled into the cabin of the truck — off to drop Tuyen off and get a free feed at her family's Vietnamese restaurant.